THE LAWYER IS LIFELESS

A HUMOROUS PARANORMAL COZY MYSTERY

CARLY WINTER

WESTWARD PUBLISHING / CARLY FALL, LLC

THE LAWYER IS LIFELESS

Even the law couldn't save him from an untimely death…

When Bernie's business meeting turns into the discovery of her murdered lawyer, she's able to uncover facts the police can't. With the help of her ghostly grandmother, Ruby, she spies on the wife and girlfriend of the deceased and also discovers a clue that may lead to proof of a local biker gangs' involvement in the killing.

Bernie's former boyfriend, Deputy Adam Gallagher, is forced to reveal a secret about the investigation—a twist Bernie could never have imagined. They decide to pool their information and work together to solve the case, but will they rekindle their romance?

After Bernie's life is threatened, she and her ghost must uncover the evidence to put the killer behind bars… or Bernie may be the next victim.

CHAPTER 1

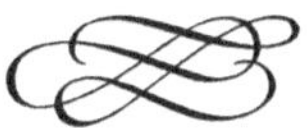

"THIS IS RIDICULOUS!" I shouted at Ruby, the ghost of my dead grandmother. We stood in the kitchen of my bed and breakfast and I waved the letter from the IRS above my head, then slammed it down on the granite countertop. "How in the world am I supposed to pay this?"

She shrugged. "I don't know, honey. I wish I hadn't spent all my money like a drunken sailor while I was alive so I had more to leave you. I don't have many regrets in life, but that's certainly becoming one of them."

I looked down at the tax bill and groaned. "What am I going to do?"

"Well, first, I think you should start taking cash. You don't have to report cash to Uncle Sam."

"Yes, you do!" I said. "It's illegal not to!"

Ruby shrugged. "Well, it could also be classified as *keeping what's yours*, but you and I tend to look at things a little differently. Tomato, tom-ah-to, and all that."

"Do you have any advice that falls into the legal realm?" I asked, rolling my eyes. Ruby had never been a rule-follower while living, nor was she in death.

"Perhaps you should look into restructuring your business. That may offer some tax benefits," she replied, tapping her finger against her lips.

Finally, an idea that sounded legal. "Where would I get that done?"

"I knew a lawyer while I was still kicking. Stanley Jones III. Nice guy. He did some work for me."

"Like what?" I asked, picking up my phone and typing in his name.

"A little of this, a little of that. Just tell him who you are and he'll see you right away."

After dialing, I waited for an answer. Had Ruby slept with the man or had they truly had a working association?

"Did you have a relationship with him?" I asked.

She shook her head and tossed her gray ponytail over her shoulder. "Heck, no. Stanley was married and I didn't sleep with married men. Well, except that one guy, but that was so long ago, it might as well never have happened. Stanley also fell out of the ugly tree at birth and hit every branch on the way down. Not my type. You know I like the hotties. Nice guy though."

I cringed listening to my seventy-something year old dead grandmother discuss "hotties."

"Stanley Jones and Associates," the pleasant woman's voice answered. "This is Penny."

"Hi, Penny. My name's Bernadette Maxwell. I need some help restructuring my business for tax purposes, and I was told Mr. Jones could help me."

"Of course. Let me see when we can get you in. Please hold."

Elevator music played as I sighed.

"Drop my name," Ruby said. "Penny knows me well. I bet you'll have an appointment this afternoon or tomorrow."

Penny came back on the line. "Does next week work for you?"

I glanced at Ruby. I hated the idea of waiting that long. With this tax bill hanging over my head, my anxiety would be through the roof and all I'd do is worry about how I would pay it. I needed to *act*. "Well, I was hoping to get in a little earlier if possible. I found his name in my grandmother's papers. Ruby—"

"You're Ruby's granddaughter?" Penny asked.

"Yes."

"Hold, please."

I narrowed my gaze at my ghost. "What's the deal with you and this office?"

She shrugged. "I brought them a lot of business."

"Bernadette?" Penny said.

"You can call me Bernie."

"Well, Bernie, Mr. Jones has an opening today at two. Will that work for you?"

"Yes. Thank you. I'll see you then."

Hanging up the phone, I narrowed my gaze at my ghost. It shouldn't surprise me dropping my grandmother's name would open doors in this town. She'd been sort of a legend, especially in the sheriff's office. "I'd love to know the story of why your name gets me a same day appointment."

"I told you, I brought him a lot of business. Jezzy's grandma, Janis, and the guy who used to own Plates of Pancakes when it was around... I used to be a big deal in this town, Bernie."

"Okay. Well, I have to be there at two."

"Can't wait to see old Stanley again!" she squealed.

"OH, LOOK!" Ruby said as we pulled out of my back lot on the way to the lawyer's office. "They took down the For Sale sign on that house over there. It must have sold! I wonder who your new neighbor will be?"

I hadn't known the last couple to live there except to wave and say hello if we found ourselves outside at the same time. They'd moved out a few weeks ago. "I have no idea."

"Maybe it'll be some hot guy who likes to do yardwork shirtless," Ruby said, sighing. "Wouldn't that be nice?"

I didn't bother to answer. My potential new neighbor was the least of my worries.

Ruby and I drove to a group of houses that had been converted into office buildings. She spun around in circles next to me as I strode through the parking lot. With Thanksgiving just two weeks away, the air felt downright wintery, so I pulled my coat around me tighter. People always associated Arizona with extreme heat, but those of us up in the mountains experienced snow during the winter months while those in the valley finally emerged from their long, hot summer to tepid temperatures.

I pushed open the front door and found an empty desk and three blue office chairs in the reception area that used to be a living room. The walls had been painted eggshell white and decorated with pictures of the Sedona skies during monsoon season: lightning, rolling black clouds, torrential rains and dust storms.

"These are amazing photos," I murmured as Ruby and I studied them.

"Janis took a lot of these," she said. "We used to grab a bottle of tequila and go out to the desert during the storms, so she could snap pictures."

I wouldn't be able to take such beautiful photos sober, let alone after drinking tequila. It seemed like Mother Nature had posed for each picture, lining up her lightning rods over the cliffs or swirling her clouds into perfect mosaics of black and grey. Beautiful, but angry and scary. "I'm impressed. If Janis took these, what are they doing here?"

"Stanley did some legal work for the bar and this was how she paid him. She could get a couple hundred Benjis per picture."

"Seriously?"

"Yup." She turned to face the reception area. "You better pound on a desk or something to get someone out here. If I remember right, Penny's got a bit of a hearing problem."

"Hello?" I called.

"You know, I've been thinking about you and Adam," Ruby started.

"There's nothing to think about," I muttered. "I don't want to talk about it."

I had successfully avoided my ex-boyfriend for the past month. Not that he'd come looking for me, but we hadn't seen each other. Slowly, my heart had begun to mend. I still regretted breaking into his condo and going through his work files, but I also was happy to see my friend Darla doing so well. She'd reopened the diner and she and Jack were spending a lot of time together. If I hadn't broken into Adam's condo, she may have returned to the psychiatric ward and into the dark places her schizophrenia took her.

"Well, I want to go see Ned."

"I'm sorry, Ruby," I whispered, hoping no one was eavesdropping. "I can't do that."

"You could stand outside Adam's door while I say hello," she replied. "I miss that crochety old cowboy and imagine how lonely he is!"

Ned, Adam's ghost, had been alone for

decades and he said he preferred the quiet. I didn't worry about him not having Ruby around in the least bit. He may be enjoying his peace.

Crossing my arms over my chest, I shook my head. No way was I going to get within a mile of Adam's condo.

"I think it would—"

"Just stop right there," I hissed, glancing down the hallway to make sure no one was coming. "You can't talk me into this, so stop trying."

Ruby grumbled something about bad attitudes, then turned back to the pictures.

"Hello?" I called again.

"I'm going to head back and see what's going on," Ruby said. "It's better than hanging with Miss No-Can-Do."

Since she couldn't go more than fifteen feet from me while we were outside our house, I stood at the mouth of the hallway so she could search as much of the building as possible. What I longed to do was take off out the front door and have our tether snap her back behind me simply because she hated when I did it. Yet, this was no place to start a fight and I did need to find out how to lower my dang taxes.

"No one in the kitchen," she said as she appeared from the entrance to the left. Moving across the hall, she ghosted through a door.

"Looks like he's got himself a partner," Ruby said after returning to the hallway. "That room used to be storage, but now there's a messy desk and some file cabinets." She motioned me to follow her. "Come down here a ways. I'm at the end of my leash."

With a quick glance, I sought out security cameras. Having been caught in the act of breaking and entering, not to mention going through Adam's police files, I now hunted the corners of every building I entered in search of them. I didn't see anything in the lawyer's office.

I took a few steps and peeked around the corner at the empty kitchen. The coffee pot was on and dirty dishes littered the sink.

"Come on, Bernie!" Ruby said. "You're holding me back!"

As I inched up the hallway, I passed a

bathroom door also on my left. Then another room to the right which held a large wooden table and some filing cabinets—a meeting room of sorts.

More monsoon pictures decorated the walls detailing the fury of Mother Nature. Angry black clouds, fingers of lightning bolts, streams from torrential rains where hard, desert land had been only moments before. My heart thumped loudly as I stared at one particularly fierce photo and it suddenly felt as if that storm was coming alive right in this small home.

"What's your problem?" Ruby chided. "We still have to check this back room. We'll probably find old Stanley in here on the toilet or something."

I glanced back at the front door. Where had everyone gone? At two o'clock in the afternoon on a Wednesday, I expected a lawyer's office to be busy. Where was Penny, the receptionist? And why was the coffee pot on if no one was here?

"I have a bad feeling about this," I whispered. "I think we should leave."

"No. We've got one more room to investigate. I'm sure Stanley just stepped out for a minute or he's in the bathroom. He's even deafer than Penny. She probably took a late lunch."

I hesitantly moved closer to the doorway and Ruby was able to slip in. She immediately returned.

"Uh oh," she said. "We have a problem."

"What? What's wrong?"

"The lawyer... he's lifeless. Stanley's dead. You better call 9-1-1."

The storm brewed louder, causing a buzzing sound in my head. "Are you kidding me?"

"Nope." She gestured to the room. "Take a look."

I hurried inside. The far wall held a half-dozen file cabinets. Stanley sat behind his big, oak desk, his head leaned against the back of the chair, his eyes closed. If not for his blue lips and fingers, I would've guessed he was resting.

"He looks like he's napping," I whispered.

"Honey, he's in for the longest sleep of

his life. There's no waking up from that one."

Instead of checking for a pulse, I nodded and stepped back into the hallway. "I have to call the police."

"Yup. That's what I told you."

My heart thundered as I strode out into the reception area. With shaky hands, I pulled out my phone from my purse and dialed. I knew from experience blue lips meant possible poisoning. I had the drug dealer who died in my upstairs room to thank for that unwanted piece of knowledge.

After being told someone would be sent out right away, I debated whether to wait outside. I stood in the middle of reception and tried to occupy my thoughts with the pictures once again instead of the dead body in back.

"Come down the hallway," Ruby said. "I want to look around."

"No. I'm waiting right here for the police."

"If you stand in the hallway, you can still see out the window and you'll know when the police have arrived. You'll also make your poor, dead grandmother happy."

I cursed under my breath as I glanced at her. She stood fifteen feet away with a sweet smile on her face, her hands clasped in front of her as if she were a saint.

"Fine," I muttered. Sirens wailed in the distance. "Make this fast, Ruby." I placed myself in the middle of the hallway, which gave me good views of both the front door and Stanley's office where Ruby had disappeared.

After a few moments, a police cruiser pulled up. "They're here," I called. "I'm going back to the reception." Ruby yelped as our tether snapped her back toward me while I strode toward the front door.

"I hate when you do that."

"I know." And it was exactly why I enjoyed it.

As I stared out the window, I prayed Adam hadn't caught the call. The glare of the car window prevented me from getting a glimpse of who was behind the wheel.

"Please don't be Adam," I whispered.

"Of course it's going to be Adam," Ruby

countered, standing next to me. "That's exactly the type of luck you have."

I didn't want to see my ex-boyfriend, especially at a murder scene and after I'd successfully avoided him for a month.

The car door opened. A man stepped out. My heart sank when he turned to study the office building. After running a hand through his blond hair, he pushed his sunglasses up his nose.

Ruby snickered. "See? I told you."

It was Adam.

CHAPTER 2

AS ADAM STRODE up the walkway, I whispered, "You are an adult. Act like one." Which meant I wouldn't hide under Penny's desk like I wanted to.

I smiled when he entered. As he slipped off his glasses, his eyes widened in surprise. He quickly settled his features into what I called his cop face and nodded at me. All business.

"Bernie. What are you doing here?"

"I found the body," I said, my heart thundering as I tucked a stray lock of black hair behind my ear. How I longed to be held in his arms and have him kiss the tip of my nose.

He sighed and shook his head. "Why are you at this office?"

"I had an appointment today at two. When I arrived, no one was here. Well, I thought no one was here. Then I looked around and found the lawyer."

"Where is he?"

"Back there," I replied, pointing down the hallway.

"You're sure he's dead?"

"He's blue," I said, shrugging. "I didn't check for a pulse, though."

Adam glanced outside, then shut the door. "Is Ruby here?"

"Tell him no!" she yelled. "I want to sneak around a little bit more!"

Shaking my head, I replied, "I left her at home." Perhaps I should have felt guilty lying to the police during a possible murder investigation, but I didn't. If Ruby wanted to prowl around, why should I care? It wasn't like she was going to contaminate the scene, and I was the only one who could hear or see her.

"Good," Adam said. "Come show me exactly what you did before you found him."

"I'll stay away from him so he doesn't smell me." Ruby's distinct scent consisted of lavender and marijuana, and Adam would recognize it in a second.

As I retraced my steps, I mentioned the coffee pot being left on and the dirty dishes in the sink. "It seems like everyone but Stanley left in a hurry."

He nodded as he followed me down the hallway. "Did you open this door?" he asked, pointing at the closed panel Ruby said held another office.

"No."

Adam peeked in and shut it again. "Then you went into that room down there?"

He motioned toward Stanley's office and I nodded.

"Come on, Bernie," Ruby urged. "I was in the middle of reading something before the copper got here. I want to finish it!"

I walked toward Stanley's office and stopped in the doorway. Ruby circled around the desk and stood next to Stanley, staring at the computer.

"Well, I'll be darned," she muttered, shaking her head as Adam pulled out a set of rubber gloves from his pocket and slipped them on. Ruby stepped away and returned to my side as he laid his fingers on the victim's neck, searching for a pulse.

"Yuck," she said as we watched him. "Dead people are gross."

"He's gone," Adam concluded. "If you could step back into the reception area, I'd appreciate it."

I nodded and strode back down the hallway, taking a seat in one of the blue chairs by the front door.

"He's so serious," Ruby said. "I thought he'd be dropping on his knees begging you to come back."

I didn't answer. My focus was on Adam's voice. I couldn't hear what he said, but deep rumblings filtered down the hall.

A few moments later, he returned to the reception and leaned up against the desk. "The sheriff is on his way."

"Okay. Should I stick around?"

"Yup." He crossed his arms over his chest. We sat in silence for long moments, each one becoming more uncomfortable than the last. I took up studying my cuticles. "How are things going, Bernie?"

I miss you. Some days I don't want to get out of bed. I'm sorry for what I did and that I broke your trust. Please forgive me. "Everything's fine."

He nodded and kept his gaze on me. "Is business good?"

"Yes. Fine. Thanks for asking." I went back to my cuticles. I hated that word. Fine. It was so… vanilla. And I unintentionally used it when things weren't great but I didn't want anyone to know.

"I… uh… I've been thinking about you."

My head snapped up so quickly, my neck cracked. Had I heard that right? His features had softened slightly, so maybe I had.

"Old lover boy's back in action!" Ruby yelled. "Woohoo!"

"What did you say?" I asked, waving my hand to shush my ghost.

Sirens wailed outside and I silently cursed them.

"I better go tell the ambulance they

aren't needed," Adam said. "Please stay where you are."

His cop face returned as he strode out the door.

"Did he say he's been thinking about me?" I whispered.

"He sure did," Ruby said, grinning. "He's coming around, realizing he can't live without the hotel hottie."

"Really? The hotel hottie?"

"The bed and breakfast bedazzler?"

I rolled my eyes. "Just please be quiet."

Adam strode inside again, this time accompanied by Sheriff Walker.

"Well, well, well," he said, tipping his cowboy hat in my direction. "Bernadette Maxwell as I live and breathe. Why am I not surprised?"

"Hello, Sheriff," Ruby said. "I'd love to come over and get in your face, but I'm not supposed to be here."

I shrugged and smiled. "I had an appointment at two. I found him."

"I'm sure you did. Lead the way, Adam," Walker said. "Let's see old Stanley."

The two men disappeared down the

hallway. Ruby stood and walked away from me to the end of our tether. "Get up. Come stand by the kitchen."

"No," I whispered.

"Come on! I want to snoop in this other lawyer's office."

"No!" I hissed. "Stop it right now!"

"I have a plan, Bernie," Ruby said. "Now, get off your tush and help me help you."

With a sigh, I stood and ambled over. I had no idea what she meant, but if me loitering in the hallway kept her quiet, I'd do it.

Ruby ghosted through the closed door, giving me the opportunity to eavesdrop on the police.

"The blue lips and fingers are a dead giveaway, excuse my pun," Sheriff Walker stated. "This isn't a natural death."

"Poisoning?" Adam asked.

"That's my guess, but forensics will have to verify it."

Oh, heck. Another murder? I rubbed my temples to try to ward off the headache forming behind my eyes.

"Do you think she's got anything to do

with it?" the sheriff asked. Since I was the only "she" in the building, I had to assume he spoke of me.

"I don't know," Adam said.

Whispering a curse, I couldn't believe the audacity of my former boyfriend. He hadn't seen me in a month and now I could possibly be involved in a murder? Jerk.

"Well, let's take a look around while we're waiting for the coroner," Walker said. "Keep your eyes open for anything suspicious."

I hurried back to my chair with a yelping Ruby fluttering behind me. Just as I sat down, the two men emerged from the hallway.

Trying to avoid their glares, I returned to studying my cuticles.

"I'm just going to put my cute little old self in this corner over here," Ruby said as Adam approached. She moved beside the potted plant.

Adam hovered over me while the sheriff searched Penny's desk.

"Tell us again. What time was your appointment?" he asked, retrieving his pen and notepad from his back pocket.

"Two."

He glanced over at the sheriff who was flipping through a paper calendar on Penny's desk. "Confirmed."

"And no one was here when you arrived?"

"No. I thought someone was maybe in back and couldn't hear me, so I did a quick search and found Stanley."

"Well, I'll be darned," Sheriff Walker said. He held up a small bottle with clear liquid. "Look at this."

"What's that?" Ruby asked.

"Eye drops," Walker muttered. "Otherwise known as Tetrahydrozoline. Very lethal when orally ingested. And half the bottle is gone."

"Is that in Penny's desk?" Adam asked.

"Yup. Tossed here right on top, which is a bit off considering the rest of the drawer is immaculate."

I tried to pretend I wasn't listening, but I stared at the bottle until Walker set it down. Eye drops. I'd used them many times for allergies and never known they could be fatal. Recalling the coffee cup on Stanley's desk, I wondered if that was how the toxic substance had been delivered. But who had poisoned him and why?

Just then, the front door swung open.

"What's going on here?" the man asked. In his thirties with a headful of black hair, his biceps strained against his yellow golf shirt and his black slacks seemed a little tight around his thick thighs. He obviously spent a lot of time in the gym.

The sheriff walked around the desk and stood directly in front of him. "Who are you?"

"Ricky Summers. I work here. What's going on?"

"Stanley Jones is dead," Adam said. "Can you please sit down and tell me where you've been?"

Ricky stared at Adam for a long moment, then shook his head. "I'm sorry Stanley's dead, but I've got work to do."

"Sir, this looks to be a murder investigation, so we would appreciate your full cooperation." Adam pointed to the chair next to me. "Now please. Sit."

"He's kind of sexy when he gets all bossy like that," Ruby sighed. "But he's learning from the best. Old Bruce is the bossiest man I've ever known."

My dead grandmother referring to my ex-boyfriend as sexy turned my stomach as much as her discussing "hotties."

"A murder investigation! Stanley was murdered?" He slowly lowered himself into the chair, his eyes wide. "Who are you?" he asked me.

"Bernie."

"What are you doing here? Are you the killer?"

Ruby burst out laughing and bent over, clutching her gut. "This guy's stupid. Anyone could take one look at your pretty face and know you're more harmless than me."

"No," I said sweetly. "I had an appointment with Stanley today. I found him."

"How did he die? Did someone shoot him? Knife him? Beat him with a club?"

I glanced at Adam who had narrowed

his gaze on Ricky. "Let's just sit quietly for now," he growled. "We'll get your statement soon, Mr. Summers."

As Ricky and I remained shoulder-to-shoulder, I wished there was somewhere else for me to be. He gave me the creeps but I couldn't figure out why.

"As a general rule, I hate lawyers," Ruby said. "Except for the ones that are working for me. But even then, they can't be trusted. They can turn on a dime."

I didn't bother bringing up client/attorney privilege or those pesky rules of ethical conduct that kept lawyers from flipping on their clients.

The sheriff and Adam greeted the coroner and his assistant when they entered and then the four of them made their way back to the body where they spoke in low tones.

"I don't have time for this," Ricky muttered. "I've got things to attend to." He hurried into his office and quietly shut the door. I almost yelled for Adam, but decided to mind my own business. Ricky seemed far more troubled about the fact his day had been interrupted than the reality his boss was gone.

When he returned a few moments later, I asked, "Are you even a little upset that Stanley's dead? You two did work together."

He shrugged. "I've been trying to get him to retire for a couple of months now. He was past his prime."

I stared at him incredulously and didn't bother to attempt to close my slacked jaw. How could he be so crass?

"Look at Penny's desk," he continued. I glanced over to where he pointed. "That old bat still uses a paper calendar to keep track of all our appointments. I'd brought it up more than once that things could be streamlined if we took the scheduling on-line, but neither Penny nor Stanley wanted anything to do with it. How archaic. Right from the Stone Age. Dang tree killers."

I found technology helpful in my own business, but to each their own. "So? If things ran smoothly, what did it matter how they did it?"

"Now I can do what I want with the office," Ricky replied. "I was made partner not too long ago. I've got big plans."

"Like what?" Ruby asked. I repeated her question.

"The first thing I'm going to do is fire Penny. She's been here thirty years and is worthless."

"Big plans from the big boy," Ruby muttered. "Poor Penny isn't going to be happy."

Adam emerged from the hallway. "Bernie, you can go. Ricky, you'll need to stay so we can get your statement."

I stood, happy to be leaving, but I was also curious to find out if Adam had opened a door to a possible reconciliation between the two of us.

Ruby trailed behind me quiet as an empty church until we got into the car. Just as we were pulling out, she pointed at another vehicle that had turned into the parking lot. "That's Penny," she said.

I glanced at the woman in her sixties staring at the building with wide eyes. Short, curly gray hair framed her pudgy face.

"She looks a little pale." Ruby shook her

ghostly head. "Wait until she actually gets inside. She's going to lose her mind."

We drove toward home in silence. "I want to have a meeting of the two great minds," Ruby said after a while. "That's you and me, in case you were wondering."

"About what?"

"Stanley's murder. I have an idea."

Oh, no.

Nothing good ever came from one of Ruby's plans.

CHAPTER 3

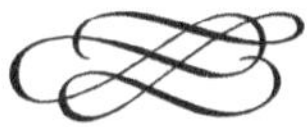

WHEN WE ARRIVED at my empty house, I hung my coat and scarf on a peg by the back door and threw some logs into the fireplace along with some newspaper and wood clippings. As the fire roared to life, I stood in front of the flames and watched them dance. The heat quickly warmed the room and both Ruby and I plopped down on the sofa with a sigh. Elvira, my cranky tabby, strolled downstairs and curled up against Ruby. She never explored the house when we had guests, but when it was just the three of us, she liked to survey the back parking lot and the desert beyond it from the upstairs windowsill at the end of the hallway. Bunnies, geckos and other wildlife held her attention for hours.

I had one couple staying with me and they'd informed me the prior night they'd be on a long day hike and wouldn't be back until late. Until then, I, my ghost, and my cat would enjoy the house to ourselves.

"I always loved sitting in front of the fire like this when I was alive," Ruby said wistfully as she stared at the leaping flames. "I wish I could feel the warmth on my face."

"It feels nice." Once again, I was sad my grandmother was trapped and could no longer enjoy the things she used to love. "What did you want to talk about?" I asked, setting my phone on the cushion beside me.

"The murder."

"Why?"

"Because I found some really interesting things while I was snooping around."

"Really? Like what?"

"There's some shady stuff going on in that office."

Logically, I should rise from the couch and proceed with my day. However, curiosity seemed to rule the roost once again.

And the fire did feel really nice. I sank deeper into the cushions as relaxation swept through me. "What's that?"

"Well, first let's discuss what old Stanley was doing when he bit the big one."

"Okay... "

"He wasn't emailing his wife, but his girlfriend."

I arched an eyebrow. "And you saw this on his computer?"

"Yup. I knew his wife when I was alive. Her name's Ann. She's a nice woman—a bit of a doormat, but pleasant. The email was addressed to Merry at Joyous Jewels. Isn't that the place where you bought the mood ring I loved so much that you lost?"

Yes, the mood ring. Ruby had convinced me to buy the jewelry months ago and I'd misplaced it. The fact I'd lost the ring she adored seemed to bother her quite a bit because she kept bringing it up.

I recalled the woman who had helped us at the store. She'd reminded me of a younger Ruby with her long blonde hair and flowing skirts. Her with Stanley? Who had probably been in his seventies? No way. Ruby had to be mistaken.

"Just to clarify, you're telling me that Stanley was having an affair with the woman at the jewelry store?"

"Yup. Unless there's another store in town named Joyous Jewels."

I shook my head. "What did the email say?"

"It was a follow-up email. He had sent one a couple of days ago saying their relationship was over. He had taken the email he sent previously, then added to it, telling her he missed her and he'd changed his mind. He couldn't live without her."

"But the most recent email was never sent?"

"Nope. Only the one ending the relationship."

"Huh. They're a strange pairing."

"Oh, yeah. Probably one of convenience, as those types often are."

"Those types?"

"An old guy and a young, beautiful woman."

Of course I'd heard of such relationships, but I wasn't sure convenience was the correct word to describe these arrangements. Stanley had to sneak around on his wife and I assumed Merry was sleeping with him, which held a pretty big yuck factor in my book. Stanley hadn't exactly been some silver fox—a bald head, protruding belly, and more wrinkles than a Shar-Pei puppy. Why would she go to bed with him? Seemed more trouble than it was worth, especially for Merry. Besides, I didn't even know if the woman who had waited on me the day I bought the mood ring *was* Merry. Perhaps another woman worked at the store, one closer to Stanley's age.

"I'm sure the police will question whoever Merry is," I said.

"You bet your bottom they will," Ruby replied. "My guess is she doesn't have much to say to them."

"Why?"

"To keep her name in the clear. So Ann doesn't find out."

"Ann probably already knows."

"Uh, I don't know, Bernie. Stanley always had trouble keeping his zipper in the upright position. Either Ann is as ignorant as they come or she just turns a blind eye. Like I said, she's kind of a doormat."

"What else did you find?" I asked.

Ruby smiled like a Cheshire cat. "Good stuff."

I should've walked away and minded my own business. But Ruby always had a way of sucking me in. "Spill it."

"Ricky's an interesting character," she said, stroking Elvira. Her hand wafted right through the cat's head, but the feline seemed to enjoy the attention as she purred loudly. "Do you remember when he was told to sit and then he went into his office?"

I nodded. "I should've yelled for Adam."

"No, I'm glad you didn't because I can't wait to find out how this plays out. I think he was getting rid of evidence."

"Are you saying Ricky killed Stanley?" I asked. "What did you see?"

"I'm saying it could very well be a possibility. While I was snooping around in there, I found some interesting things. For starters, Ricky was making plans to take the practice in a different direction."

I furrowed my brow and shook my head. "What does that mean?"

"Stanley was always a pretty straightforward guy. Likes to stick to law that doesn't get messy, like wills and businesses. Real snoozer stuff. He hated criminal law, which is why he'd never represented me when I was arrested. I always had to go to someone else. Ricky, it seems, wanted to breathe fresh life into the practice."

"By doing what?"

"Apparently, he had plans to dive into the criminal law field. There was an open file about a biker trial."

"Bikers! Like the Moonlit Coffin gang?"

"Exactly."

The Moonlit Coffin gang pretty much kept to themselves, but they were a presence in the Sedona area. Especially on weekends, their motorcycles could often be heard rumbling through the streets. I didn't know any of the members, nor had I had any interaction with any. I did see members in the grocery store wearing the gangs biker cut buying a case of beer every now and then, but I never spoke to them.

"They like to hang out at Tip 'Em Back," Ruby said. "Jezzy was actually dating the number two in the club, but I don't know if she still is."

None of what Ruby told me should surprise me, but for some reason, it most certainly did. It had never occurred to me that Jezebel could be dating a member of a motorcycle gang, but it fit. With her tattoos and rough disposition, such a man would be a perfect match. "Why wasn't I aware of any of this?"

Ruby shrugged. "We've never been to Tip 'Em Back at night, Bernie. You always want to read or watch a bit of television. We're at home when the bikers come out to play."

Okay, she had a point. I couldn't recall the last time I'd been out of the house after eight in the evening. Probably when I dated Adam, and we never visited Tip 'Em Back.

"So, anyway, Ricky was taking a case for one of the Moonlit Coffin members," Ruby continued. "My guess is he was doing it on the down-low so Stanley wouldn't find out."

"What was the case?"

"Assault."

"Who was the accused?"

"His name was Spike."

"Is that his real name? Who in the world would call their kid that?"

"Probably not. All the bikers have different nicknames they go by. I didn't see a real name."

"So you think Ricky killed Stanley because of the case?"

"I think there's a *chance* that Ricky killed him because of the case. He had notes in his office about changing the mission of the practice. He's the lone partner now, so he can do what he wants. Unless Stanley's wife owns part of the practice. I don't know how those things work."

Interesting. If Ricky wanted sole ownership of the office, would he have to get rid of Ann next? Or perhaps Ann wanted her husband gone not because he was cheating, but so she could pull the strings in the law firm and have control over the bank accounts?

I stared at Ruby for a long moment. "What if Stanley had found out about the case and told him to drop it? What if Ricky killed him because of it?"

"Or what if Ricky had someone from Moonlit Coffin murder him?" Ruby mused.

Shaking my head, I pursed my lips. "I bet you're right. Ricky went back into his office to hide his plans and the file about the case."

"The police will probably never find out about it," Ruby said.

"Probably not."

"But *we* know about it," she stressed, still grinning.

"So? What do you want to do with the information?"

"Well, my guess is if the cops do find out about Ricky's plans and the case, they're going to have a chat with some members of Moonlit Coffin. Bikers don't talk to police. Jezebel won't speak to the cops either, regardless of whether she's dating a biker or not."

I still didn't follow. "And?"

"This is your chance to get Adam back," Ruby said.

"How in the world did you make that jump?" I asked, rolling my eyes.

"I have a plan."

"You know I hate it when you say that."

"Yes, but it's perfect."

"I thought you didn't like me dating Adam."

Ruby sighed. "I thought you'd be over him by now, but you aren't. You mope around here like you're carrying the weight of five semi-trucks on your shoulders. Adam's not a bad guy, especially for a cop. I want to see you happy, and he did that for you. So now, we have to win him back."

"Ruby, that's just—"

"Nope," she cut in, raising her hand. "Just hear me out. He said he's been thinking about you. We're going to turn his world upside down so not only does he think about you, but he sees you often and realizes he can't live—or solve this case— without you."

I stared at my grandmother as my heart hammered. Getting back together with Adam? *Count me in.* But I couldn't *make* him care about me again. I had no idea what she had up her sleeve.

"How are we going to pull this off?" I asked.

"Trust your old grandma," Ruby said with a wink. "Like I mentioned, I have a plan."

CHAPTER 4

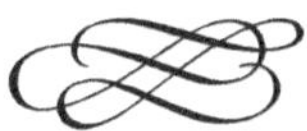

THE NEXT MORNING, Darla quietly tapped on my back door. As she entered carrying a quiche and some cinnamon buns, my mouth watered. We used to have an arrangement where she'd prepare breakfast for my customers, but that had fallen by the wayside for a while. She was back at it and I was happy to be able to advertise an excellent home-cooked meal for my travelers—one that I didn't have to attempt to make.

With a groan, I eyed the bacon and cheese quiche.

"Before you eat everything yourself, you better set it in the oven on warm," she said.

Good point. Out of sight, out of mind.

"Do you want some coffee?" I offered as I turned the oven dial and slid in the quiche and cinnamon buns. My guests had yet to make a sound and I assumed the long hike yesterday had worn them out.

"Sure." She pulled out a small, glass bottle from her coat pocket and set it on the counter. I immediately recognized it—Darla's homemade flavoring for coffee. "I'm trying to figure out the best way to market this stuff. And to name it. I can't market it without a name."

The nutmeg, cinnamon and vanilla concoction was my new favorite addition to my morning coffee and I was happy Darla was offering it at the diner. If she could get it placed on store shelves, the yumminess would take off and become very popular. "Have you talked to the grocery store yet?" I asked as I scooped the grounds into the coffee maker. "What about Canyon Coffee?"

"I haven't," she said with a sigh.

"Why?"

She pursed her lips. "I don't like the idea of them telling me no."

As I was about to launch into a speech about positive thinking, I decided to let it slide. Darla had come so far in such a short period of time. With her schizophrenia under control, her diner was once again beginning to thrive. She and Jack, the owner of Jumpin' Jack Jeep Tours, were dating and she seemed happy and content. Domination of the tasty coffee world could wait until she was more confident. Instead of lecturing, I poured in the water and hit the brew button.

I turned to my friend and smiled. "When you're ready, let me know if there's anything I can do to help you," I said, squeezing her fingers. "Let me get your payment for today."

As I rummaged through my purse, she asked, "Did you read the paper this morning?"

Darla was the only person I knew who still had the paper delivered every morning. I read mine digitally, but had only glanced at it today. I had a feeling what she was about to mention but decided to let her take the lead. "No. What happened?"

"My lawyer was discovered dead," she said. "Stanley Jones."

I nodded and handed her the money. "I didn't know he was your lawyer."

"Yes. He took care of some business items for me. He was a good guy."

That seemed to be the consensus. Time to let the cat out of the bag, so to speak. "I found the body," I said, hoping it didn't upset her too much.

Darla's eyes widened. "Wow, Bernie. That shouldn't surprise me, but for some reason, it does. What were you doing there?"

The coffee pot hissed and gurgled, alerting me it had produced its final product. "I had an appointment to see him about restructuring my business for tax purposes," I replied as I retrieved two cups and poured. "I got a tax bill much bigger than I expected and I'm not too happy about it."

Darla took the cup from me and blew on the liquid. "Is anyone ever happy about paying taxes?"

"No, probably not," I replied, chuckling.

"Well, it's too bad about Stanley." Darla

scooped her flavor concoction into her coffee and stirred, then passed the spoon to me. "He was a good guy."

I didn't want to mention that Stanley might have been murdered. However, the evidence pointed toward it and the sheriff had mentioned it more than once. I still wasn't on board with Ruby's grand master plan to get Adam and me back together, but there wasn't any reason why I couldn't gather a little information. If anyone was familiar with the Moonlit Coffin biker gang besides Jezebel, it would be Darla. I'd seen them at the diner more than once.

"Darla, what can you tell me about the Moonlit Coffin biker club?"

She shrugged. "They come in frequently. Very polite. Always tip well. They're scary looking but are always nice to me and my staff."

It certainly didn't sound like a bunch who would murder a lawyer. Besides, wouldn't a gang beat him to death, or use a weapon? The sheriff had indicated Stanley had died from poisoning. With eyedrops. Not very gang-ish to me.

"Jack works on their bikes every now and then," Darla said. "Why do you ask?"

Here's where things got tricky. Darla didn't know about Ruby, so I couldn't tell her my ghost had found evidence the biker club may be involved in Stanley's death. "I just thought I overheard the sheriff mention them and I've never had any interaction with them. They aren't on my radar, so I'm curious."

"I find them interesting," she said, nodding. "They have a president. His name's Thunder. He always orders a BLT and a vanilla milkshake. The vice-president is Gunner. He likes the egg salad sandwiches and lots of coffee. After that, I'm not sure who's who. They have their own ecosystem of command and those two are always the ones who do most of the talking for the group."

Intriguing. I never imagined a biker gang to be well-organized.

"One time a while back, eight of them came in with a new guy who wanted to join. I think they called him a prospect. Anyway, he was going for laughs from the club members and was a little rude to my waitress and made some inappropriate remarks. Well, I thought the poor guy was going to end up as fertilizer when Thunder and Gunner set him straight. They made him stand up and apologize to my server and leave her a fifty-dollar tip. The next day, he also showed up with a bouquet of flowers and once again said he was sorry for his horrible behavior. They don't put up with disrespecting women."

The story made them a little less scary to me. But... hmm... turning someone into fertilizer meant killing them. "Have you seen the prospect since?"

She nodded and chuckled. "He's always really polite now."

So I couldn't link any murder to the gang at this time, but that didn't mean they didn't kill Stanley.

"Jack's way more involved with them than I am," Darla continued. "He spends hours with them when he fixes their bikes. If you have more questions, you should talk to him."

Even though Darla's experiences with

Moonlit Coffin were pleasant, that didn't mean they weren't bad people. Perhaps they played nice with the local businesses because they lived in the area. For all I knew, they were responsible for hundreds of unsolved crimes throughout Arizona.

Ruby appeared next to Darla. "Sounds like our girl is doing well. She definitely looks healthy and happy. I'm sure Mr. Dimples has something to do with that. He'd make any woman happy with those rugged good looks and that smile of his."

Speaking of... "Is everything going well between you and Jack?" I asked.

Darla sighed as a deep blush crawled up her neck. "Great. Things are really good. I've fallen for him pretty hard."

"Mr. Dimples for the win!" Ruby shouted. "I'm happy and yet, so envious of this woman here. Cuddling up to Jack every night... dang, what a score."

When Darla's nose twitched, I was confident she'd smelled Ruby's distinct scent: lavender and marijuana. Whether she would question me about it remained to be seen.

"What's on your agenda for the day?" Darla asked as she sipped her coffee.

"I've got a couple upstairs who are supposed to check out today, so I'll get their room clean. Other than that, I don't have any plans."

"Yes, you do," Ruby said. "You're going to talk to some people and gather as much information as you can to give to Adam and win back his trust and heart."

Pursing my lips, I fought the urge to reply. I hadn't agreed to Ruby's hairbrained scheme, but surprise, surprise, I was leaning toward going through with it. She had seen information in Ricky's office that the sheriff most likely hadn't. I knew things. And besides, asking a few questions here and there couldn't hurt, right?

"Bernie, I need to ask you something," Darla said, eyeing me warily while she tucked a lock of blonde hair behind her ear. "Please promise me you won't take offense."

Uh-oh. That didn't sound good. "Sure. What's up?"

"Do you smoke weed?"

Ruby cackled while waving her hands in

front of her face and yelling, "Boo!" To Darla, it probably reeked like a drug den.

"No, I don't," I muttered as Ruby moved behind my friend and danced a little jig. "Why do you ask?"

"I smell it when I'm here, and sometimes when I see you outside the house," she replied. "The odor is really strong at times."

"Booga, booga, booga!" Ruby yelled in Darla's ear. She was probably drowning in the scent.

"And there are times, like right now, where you're looking my way but you aren't looking *at* me. It's almost as if you're completely distracted. Is that the drugs?"

I sighed and ran my index finger over another headache that had begun to form right between my eyes. Ruby had a way of giving them to me so easily.

Should I tell Darla about my ghost?

As one of my best friends, I felt I owed it to her. My behavior could be strange at times and I could usually attribute that to Ruby and her shenanigans. Or her almost-constant stream of chatter. It was easy to become sidetracked with her around.

"Just tell her," Ruby urged. "She seems like she's in a stable place. I think she can handle the truth."

Darla stared at me expectantly. With a sigh, I waved for her to follow me to my bedroom. No way would I take the chance of my guests overhearing our conversation.

"What's going on?" she said as I shut the door. Elvira sprawled out in the middle of my unmade bed. Darla reached out to pet her as she sat down, but the cat jumped from the mattress and ensconced herself underneath the bed. I curled up on my rocking chair. We stared at each other for a long moment, then I said, "Did you ever know my grandmother?"

Darla had lived in town a little bit longer than me, but she shook her head. "Not that I recall."

"Oh, you'd know if you did," I muttered.

"I'm not sure whether to be flattered or offended by that comment," Ruby said, ghosting through the door. She plopped down next to Darla and smiled. "This is going to be good. I'd be crazy to miss this big reveal."

Darla took a sip of coffee. "What about her?"

For some reason, I had trouble getting the words out. They just didn't want to come. And honestly, I sometimes wondered if *I* needed some medication and therapy. What if Ruby was one big hallucination? What if me being struck by lightning had caused my brain to short-circuit and everything I'd experienced with Ruby had simply been my imagination? No one but me could see or hear her.

But then I considered times like in Stanley's office... Ruby had gone into Ricky's office and snooped around and told me what she'd found. Or had I somehow entered the space, found the information, and hallucinated Ruby sharing everything? It wasn't the first time I'd questioned my own sanity. But everyone smelled Ruby, so that had to make her real... right? I needed to stop doubting myself.

"What... what do you think happens to people after they die?" I asked.

"They go to either heaven or hell. What

does that have to do with you smoking pot?"

"I'm not smoking anything," I replied. "What you smell is my grandmother, Ruby."

Darla's brow furrowed. "Excuse me?"

"You smell marijuana and lavender, right?"

She nodded slowly.

"That's Ruby's ghost, Darla. She's stuck in this plane and neither of us know why."

CHAPTER 5

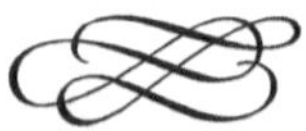

WHEN I HEARD voices in the kitchen, I jumped up from my chair. "Stay here," I whispered.

"I'm not going anywhere," Ruby said while Darla simply stared at me, wide-eyed.

As I hurried into the kitchen, I regretted spilling my secret to Darla. Not only did I worry about her mental health, but also her gossiping about me. She wouldn't spread rumors with vicious intent, but if she said something to the wrong person, the whole town would become aware I thought I hung out with my dead grandmother.

I greeted my guests and served them the quiche and cinnamon buns. We chatted for a few moments as they ate, and then they went upstairs to pack. Doing the dishes delayed my conversation with Darla. I kept my eye on the back door, fully expecting her to make her escape from me and my ghostly claims.

After my guests left, I returned to the bedroom and found Darla sitting exactly where I had left her, Ruby at her side. I lowered myself into the rocking chair.

"I think she blew a gasket," Ruby said. "She hasn't even moved."

"Darla?" I spoke softly. "Are you okay?"

She met my gaze and nodded. "I was going to leave. I mean, what you say is absolutely out of this world, Bernie, and I wasn't sure I wanted to be around you with my own mental health struggles."

"I understand. I thought—"

Darla held up her hand. "But then I remember how you were there for me even when I pushed you away. I want to do the same for you."

With a grin and sigh of relief, I said, "Thanks, Darla. I appreciate your friendship."

She nodded and took a deep breath. "Are your guests gone?"

"Yes."

"Do you have any more coffee?"

"I'll put on a fresh pot."

After the coffee had been brewed and we sat at the kitchen island, Darla fixed her gaze on me. "Tell me about Ruby."

I explained that I began seeing her after I returned from my cousin's wedding in Louisiana where I'd been hit by lightning. "She's here," I said, shrugging. "I can see and hear her. We talk all the time. I'm not sure what else to say."

"Do you... believe she's real?" Darla asked, glancing around the kitchen. "Or do you think this is a medical issue?"

"Of course I'm real," Ruby said. "As real as the sun shining."

I cleared my throat. Ruby wouldn't like what I had to say, but I had to be honest with Darla. "Sometimes I wonder if I need to visit a doctor, but most of the time, I'm certain she's stuck on this plane."

"You don't need to see a doctor, Bernie," Ruby said, rolling her eyes. "You know deep in your heart that I'm here for good. Heaven and Hell don't want me."

Darla narrowed her gaze on me. "And no one but you can hear or see her."

"Yes."

She nodded and turned to the dining room. "Where is she right now?"

"Across the island standing by the sink."

Darla spun the stool and stared in that direction. "And she's not some evil poltergeist?"

"No," I replied. "In fact, she was probably more dangerous in life than she is in death."

Ruby snorted. "You just wait until I'm dead longer. Maybe I'll acquire some poltergeist superpowers like old Nutjob Ned has."

Ned was the ghost who lived with Adam. He'd been shot and killed decades ago and could move inanimate objects. One time, he'd thrown a book and pinged me in the forehead. We'd speculated that because he'd been dead much longer than Ruby, he had developed the ability. However, I wasn't going to discuss Ned with Darla. Perhaps in the future, but I had to have her accept

Ruby before I'd mention the old cowboy with the bloodstained shirt.

"Well, at least she's harmless," Darla muttered. "I'd hate to be hanging out with a demon spirit or something."

"She's starting to get on my nerves," Ruby said, placing her hands on her hips and glaring at my friend. "Tell her I can hear her just fine and I would appreciate some courtesy."

I cleared my throat. "Ruby says she can hear you. She's a little upset about being compared to a demon."

Darla stared at me a long while, then nodded. "Fair enough. Tell her I'm sorry."

"Tell me yourself," Ruby snapped.

"The message was received," I replied, giving Ruby a quick glare.

Darla glanced around the kitchen again and shook her head. "I want proof she exists."

I stared at my friend, unsure how to give her the evidence. "What do you want me to do?"

"Don't know yet," Darla muttered, chewing her lip.

"I can see the proverbial hamster spinning in the wheel," Ruby muttered.

"Oh! I've got it!" she shrieked, pulling out her phone. "Can I get her in a picture?"

Probably not, but who was I to stop her? "Go ahead and try."

"Is she still by the sink?"

I nodded as Ruby turned to the side, lifted her purple mumu up to her knee and blew kisses to Darla.

"Make sure she gets me at a good angle," Ruby said, lowering her chin, wiggling her eyebrows and giving what I guessed was her sexy stare. Instead, she looked like she had to use the bathroom.

With a groan, I rolled my eyes as Darla snapped away while Ruby posed and flipped her ponytail like a runway model in a photo shoot. Darla scrolled through the pictures she'd taken, her brow creased with a frown.

"Nothing," she murmured, setting down her phone. "I thought you could see spirits in pictures."

"Apparently not this one," I said.

"I'm too cute," Ruby interjected. "That's why."

"What about mirrors? Isn't there something about seeing ghosts in mirrors?"

Only in the horror films. "I think you may be thinking of vampires? The fact that you *can't* see a vampire in a mirror?"

"That's right. I should've remembered that."

I stood to fetch another cup of coffee.

Darla snapped her fingers and smacked her hand down on the granite. "Wait a minute! I know what to do!"

"That girl just about restarted my old, dead heart with that outburst." Ruby laid her hand over her sternum. Mine had skipped a beat as well. Maybe more coffee was a bad idea.

"You can hear her, right?" Darla asked.

"Yes."

"Like over the phone?"

Furrowing my brow, I tried to recall a time when I'd spoken to Ruby over the phone, but none came to mind. It seemed she was always with me. But I had heard Ned in the background while talking with Adam over the phone. "I'm... I'm not sure. What did you have in mind?"

"You leave the house. I'll stay here with Ruby. You call me and Ruby can tell you what I'm doing."

It seemed like a lot of work to prove Ruby's existence, but if that was what Darla wanted, then I'd accommodate her.

"Let me grab my keys," I said.

"You don't have to go far," Darla said. "Just around the block or something."

With my phone and purse in hand, I exited the back door and headed for my SUV. Once inside, I dialed Darla and pulled out of the dirt lot.

"Where are you?" she asked.

"Down the street by the stop sign," I replied as I parked. Ruby hummed in the background.

"Okay, what am I doing?"

"She's walking upstairs," Ruby called.

I repeated the information.

"Now she's going into the Death Room."

Yes, the room where a drug trafficker had died. "You're in the first room to the right at the top of the stairs," I said.

Darla gasped. "Do you have cameras in

here, Bernie? Is that how you're seeing all this?"

"Take a look around. Do you see any?"

"You don't want cameras in these guest rooms," Ruby said. "You can't unsee some of the things I've seen. Yuck. By the way, she's sitting on the bed messing with her hair."

When I recapped, Darla swore under her breath. "I can smell her," she whispered. "I think she's sitting right next to me."

"I am!" Ruby chirped.

"There're goosebumps crawling over my arm," Darla murmured. "Is she next to me?"

Ruby cackled. "If I got any closer, I could give her tummy a rub."

"Yes, she's with you," I said.

"I don't think I like this. I'm getting scared."

"She's harmless, Darla," I replied. "You'll smell her and feel cold if she's near you, but that's it."

"Now she's running down the stairs," Ruby yelled. "I'm afraid she's going to break her neck if she doesn't slow down!"

I sighed, wishing I'd just falsely admitted

I smoked dope and never started this conversation. "Darla—"

"And she's out the front door!" Ruby yelled.

In my rearview mirror, I spotted Darla on the sidewalk staring at my house. She placed her hands on her knees as if out of breath. Turning my car around, I returned to the house and parked next to her.

"Are you okay?" I asked after exiting the vehicle.

"I think so," she said. "I freaked out there for a moment."

"Yes, I can see that."

She took a few deep breaths while I rubbed her back.

"You really do have a haunted house," she said, shaking her head. "I know past guests have said that, but I didn't believe it."

"I didn't either... not until I came back from my cousin's wedding." I glanced up and found Ruby waving at me from the doorway. I smiled and waved back, then turned my attention back to Darla. "Are you going to be okay?"

She straightened up. "Are you sure she's harmless?"

"Yes. Between you and me, even when she tries to be scary, she just looks ridiculous."

"I can't decide whether this is the coolest or scariest thing ever. I remember being cold in your house and I thought it was a draft. And the smell... I thought you were smoking weed!"

"Don't be afraid of her," I said. "And honestly, it's probably best if you don't mention her to a lot of people."

I hadn't thought too far ahead when I'd decided to reveal Ruby's existence. If Darla went around telling people my dead grandmother's ghost inhabited my house, not only would that shed a bad light on me, but I was afraid people would worry about her mental health and think she needed more medication. Should have kept my ghost to myself, but it was too late.

"Well, I better get back to the diner," Darla said. "Thank you for sharing your secret with me."

"Bye, bye!" Ruby yelled, waving.

"Ruby says goodbye," I said. "She's standing at the doorway waving to you."

Darla glanced down the walkway and stared at the space for a long moment, then broke out into a wide grin. "Bye, Ruby! I'll see you soon!"

"Woohoo!" Ruby danced a little jig, obviously thrilled someone else knew of her existence and acknowledged her.

Wasn't that what we all wanted? To be seen, to be heard? Apparently, even in death this was true... at least for Ruby.

As Darla walked away, I returned to the house. Once I shut the door, I sighed and leaned my head against it. A weight had been lifted from me by telling Darla about Ruby, just as it had been when I shared the same with Adam. I no longer had to watch my every word or concentrate on ignoring Ruby while around her. It was quite freeing.

"So, are you ready to go?" Ruby asked.

I shook my head. "I'm not sure about your plan."

"People will talk to you about things," Ruby said, crossing her arms over her chest. "They'll tell you stuff they won't share with the coppers. My plan is sheer brilliance. You go out and speak to the people we know are going to be suspects. Then you bring the information back to Adam. You give him all the leads and let him get the accolades for solving the case. In the meantime, he's so thankful that he begs you to take him back. It's really a win-win for everyone, Bernie."

"I'm not sure about this, Ruby." The plan sounded rudimentary at best and there was the chance I could push Adam away by interfering.

"Well, I do. Now go run a brush through your hair and grab your coat. I've got it all worked out. We'll go see the girlfriend first."

As I strolled to my bedroom, I wondered how one spoke to a stranger about infidelity.

CHAPTER 6

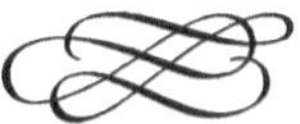

Despite the chill in the air, my hands began to sweat as we approached Joyous Jewels. I stopped just outside the door and took some deep breaths.

"Would you relax?" Ruby said. "You act like someone is dragging you to the gulag. We're going to talk to some harmless girl named Merry who sells mood rings."

I nodded and opened the door. It took a second for my eyes to adjust. Among the table displays of necklaces, rings and earrings, there wasn't a person to be found.

"Where is she?" Ruby asked. "Not that it matters. I'm heading behind the counter. Don't snap me around."

I stayed within ten feet of Ruby looking at the jewelry in the glass case as she poked around behind the counter. A replica of the mood ring I had once owned sat nestled in a white silk box. Beside it lay an array of turquoise rings and necklaces with shapes ranging from small rectangles to large ovals.

"Look at that necklace!" Ruby exclaimed, tapping the glass. The stone was so big, I imagined it could cause neck problems for its wearer. "That would look fabulous on me. With matching earrings, just call me Hot Dead Mama. You should buy it."

I shrugged and shook my head, not one for turquoise jewelry. Some women could pull it off well, but there had to be some semblance of style involved. That wasn't me, unless you counted eighties t-shirts stylish. *Back to the Future* and turquoise didn't cut it together. As I glanced up at my ghost, I didn't think purple mumus qualified as fashionable, either.

"Fine. Don't buy it," Ruby sulked. She loved living vicariously through me, but I drew the line at wearing a blue boulder around my neck. Turning back to the register, she smiled and I realized she was reading a notebook right next to it. "Well, isn't this interesting."

I didn't dare speak because someone had to be minding the store. Surely, they'd come out from the back room at any second and wonder who the heck I was talking to.

"Merry's definitely working today," Ruby said. "Either that or she's left her diary out in the open for other employees to read."

Biting my lip, I fought asking what was written in it. A diary meant a big revelation of secrets and with Ruby reading it, a definite invasion of privacy. But we were trying to gather information on a murder.

"Oh, Adam's going to love it when you tell him this."

Guilt washed through me. I wasn't trying to collect evidence for the greater good, but I had once again partaken in one of my dead grandmother's crazy schemes—this time attempting to get my boyfriend back.

"Can I help you?"

I turned to find a woman coming from the back room, her long blonde hair flowing down the sides of her red, puffy face. Her full-sleeve, floor-length light-blue dress billowed around her thin frame. As she strode behind the counter, I realized it was the same woman who had waited on me the first time I'd been in the store. She passed right through Ruby who uttered a few choice words—she didn't like people invading her space.

"Are you okay?" I blurted. The woman had obviously been crying.

"Yes," she replied, her voice firm. But then, one by one, tears cascaded down her cheeks. "No. My... someone I cared about was murdered. I'm obviously having a very hard time pulling it together."

Stanley and Merry had a relationship and the man had been killed, so I was most certainly speaking with Merry.

"I'm sorry to hear that," I said. "Would that be Stanley?"

She nodded, her eyes wide in surprise. "How did you know?"

"Well, it's the only murder I've heard about in town and I was the one who found the body."

She gasped as her cheeks paled. "Really? You found Stanley's body?"

"Yes."

"Oh, my word. Was it horrible?"

"Is finding a dead guy ever not horrible?" Ruby asked.

"It wasn't pleasant," I said. "You and Stanley were close?"

She sighed and pulled a fresh box of tissues from under the counter. "Yes, we were. He was... he was my everything."

Ruby snorted. "He was the sugar daddy. Handed out bucks to her for the store."

"I heard the police mention that he helped you with the store," I said. No such thing had ever occurred, and I guessed Ruby repeated our speculation or read it as fact in the diary.

"He did. Our relationship was... I guess... *complicated* is a perfect way to describe it."

"It may help to talk about it," I said quietly, once again feeling a bit dirty about my own selfish reasons for wanting information.

"I really can't," she whispered.

"Because he was married?" I asked, inwardly cringing. I was so far into the "this is none of my business zone," I was making myself uncomfortable.

She nodded. "Yes. He helped... finance the store. He was a sweet man who only wanted the best for me."

"Pfft," Ruby scoffed. "This one's a fat liar. Or, I should say a scrawny liar. She's not telling the truth."

I glanced over at my ghost and wondered what she'd read in the diary. Merry appeared very distraught to me. The tears were real. One couldn't fake puffy eyes.

"I'm really upset he's gone," she whispered. "I'll miss him."

Recalling that Stanley had sent an email breaking up with Merry a few days before he died, I tried to put myself in the woman's shoes. Certainly, the email would have upset her. But that didn't mean she couldn't be troubled at the man's death. If Adam died, I would be quite distressed despite the fact we hadn't seen each other in a month, except for at the murder scene.

So, yes, she could be angry he'd broken up with her, but also saddened by his passing. I wanted to ease her pain and tell her that he'd been writing an email to her before he died letting her know he didn't want to end the relationship, but I didn't know how to reveal the information without mentioning Ruby sticking her ghostly nose where it didn't belong.

Merry wiped her cheeks again. "But anyway, is there anything I can help you with? I feel like I've seen you before."

I nodded and smiled. "I bought a mood ring from you a while back."

"Of course," she said. "I couldn't place your face, but I thought I recognized you."

Glancing down at the rings again, I contemplated buying another mood ring.

"Buy it! Buy it! Buy it!" Ruby chanted.

"I misplaced it though," I said. "I can't find it anywhere. I'm not sure if it fell off or if I set it down somewhere and it got lost behind a table or something."

"That's too bad," Merry said, her brow furrowed. "Since you've been so sweet listening to me drone on about my problems, I can sell you this one at half price."

"That's really nice of you."

Merry shrugged. "I like to take care of my customers. Especially pleasant ones like you."

"So, you own the store?" I asked, keeping my gaze firmly on the ring display. I was certain I already knew the answer, but thought I'd pry a little more and confirm my suspicions.

"Yes, I do. Well, I now own it outright."

My head snapped up. "Outright? You had a partner?"

"Yes. Stanley. Like I said, he helped me with the store. He was a silent investor."

"Well, there's your motive for murder," Ruby said. "She doesn't have to sleep with the old geezer any longer and she gets the whole kit-and-kaboodle filled with all the pretty, shiny things."

Having Stanley "help with the store" as her sugar daddy was one thing, but for him to be part-owner was a whole other messy situation. And Merry was now the sole owner. Unless Stanley's portion went to his wife. My goodness, what a sticky situation. The girlfriend and the wife becoming co-owners?

Thankful I wasn't in Merry's shoes, I said, "I'll take the ring," and tapped the glass. Ruby had been correct—Merry did have a perfect motive, but I needed to think it all through so I could present Adam with hard, cold facts.

"Great!" she chirped, her tears suddenly gone. My purchase gave her happiness and took away some of the icky feelings I had.

After I paid, I slipped it on and it immediately turned black.

"Looks like you're a little stressed," Merry said. "That's what black means. Do you need another color chart?"

I nodded. "Bernie stressed? What's new?" Ruby blurted.

Merry turned and opened a drawer while I glared at my ghost.

"Here you go," she said, handing me the paper. "Hope you don't lose this one!"

"Me, too," I muttered. "Thanks again."

As I walked out of the store, a sheriff's cruiser parked about ten feet away. Adam pulled off his sunglasses and stared at me as I quickly diverted my gaze.

"Pretend you don't see him," Ruby said. "Let's go the opposite way."

I did as instructed and hurried down the sidewalk.

"He's still watching you," Ruby muttered, glancing over her shoulder. "Probably wondering what you're doing in the jewelry store."

"Bernie!"

Despite my determination to put as much space between me and Adam as possible, I came to a halt and turned. Narrowing my gaze on him, I fisted my hands at my sides as my fury flared. The jerk I was still in love with hadn't defended me when the sheriff asked him if I had anything to do with the murder.

"He's looking fit and fine in that uniform," Ruby remarked as he jogged over.

Even though I was angry, she wasn't wrong.

"What were you doing in Joyous Jewels?" he asked.

"Hello to you, too," Ruby snapped.

"I was buying a new mood ring," I replied, holding up my hand and keeping my voice even. To my utter horror, the ring had turned bright red, indicating love and passion. I quickly shoved my hand into my pocket as Ruby burst out laughing.

"Your cheeks are redder than the dang ring!" she yelled. Bending over and placing her hands on her knees, she continued to cackle at my embarrassment.

"Are you sure that's all?" Adam asked.

I sighed and rolled my eyes. "Of course it is. I liked the ring, I lost it, and I replaced it."

He narrowed his gaze on me as if trying to decide if I was lying or not. I met his stare until his softened. "Okay, Bernie. Have a great afternoon."

Scrambling to come up with an insult to get back at him for the slight with the sheriff, all I could manage was, "You too."

I hurried down the street, relieved the encounter had ended. No doubt I'd be sprawled out in bed tonight and a hundred snappy replies would filter through my mind.

"Merry did it," Ruby said.

"Why do you say that?"

"She's got an excellent motive. My guess

is she went to see Stanley that afternoon while Peggy and Ricky were at lunch. Made some fresh coffee, dumped in some eye-drops from Peggy's desk, and voilà! A dead guy and she's got the store to herself."

"But he was writing her an email when he died."

"Maybe he saw her and after she left, he realized he couldn't give up his pretty, young sidepiece."

"Perhaps," I muttered.

"And there's the little fact that, two days ago, Merry wrote in her diary that she wanted Stanley dead."

CHAPTER 7

I HAD two pieces of information the police didn't. First, Merry wanted Stanley dead bad enough she'd written it down. Second, Ricky had big plans for the law office. He wanted to move from pushing paper to representing criminals.

Well, I had to *assume* I had evidence the police didn't. Merry wouldn't be giving up her diary willingly, and Ricky had most likely buried his plans for the law office where the police wouldn't find them. However, my snoopy ghost had seen it all.

"Where are we going?" Ruby asked as I dressed the next morning. Did I go with my *Pretty in Pink* or *Top Gun* t-shirt?

I had loved the movie *Top Gun*, but for some reason, Tom Cruise had hit a nerve in the past few years, especially when he starred in the *Jack Reacher* movies. A travesty in casting, in my opinion, and frankly, it had almost ruined the books for me. I grabbed *Pretty in Pink*. Retiring the other may not be a bad idea. "I'm going to see Ricky Summers."

The fact was I still needed information on restructuring my business and I hoped Ricky would help me so I didn't have to find another lawyer. Besides, it couldn't hurt to revisit the scene of the crime.

"I'm going with you," Ruby said.

"Good. I hoped you'd say that." It was rare that I could leave the house without Ruby in tow. Sometimes, it irritated me to no end, but then I recalled her situation. I wouldn't want to be stuck in a house either. Today, I wanted her there in full-force snoop mode.

After running a brush through my long black hair, I studied my reflection in the mirror. Determined blue eyes stared back at me. In the past when I'd agreed to one of

Ruby's schemes, I'd reluctantly participated. This time, I was firm that I would bring Adam information he didn't have. Whether or not it would repair our relationship, I had no way of knowing, but I had to try. A small part of me also wanted to best the police once again and solve the murder before them... as long as it didn't involve physical altercations.

"Let's get moving," Ruby called from the kitchen. "If we hurry, we'll be the first ones in the office and he won't be able to brush us aside and claim he's too busy to talk with us."

After grabbing my purse, I headed into the kitchen and sucked down another half-cup of coffee which burned my tongue. The heat and caffeine fueled me nicely.

"Are we driving?" Ruby asked.

I pulled out my keys. "Yes. It's too cold."

"Fair enough. You know I hate walking."

"Yes, I do. You never fail to tell me every time we leave the house on foot."

Ruby chuckled and gave me a wink. "Just want to make sure you hear me loud and clear."

It was almost impossible to ignore Ruby, even when I gave it my best shot.

After locking the back door, we hurried over to my SUV and slid in. As I pulled out, I turned up the radio volume and listened to the forecast.

"Possible rain for tomorrow and through the weekend," the male voice said. "A much-anticipated drink for our environment."

"Turn that blowhard off," Ruby said, pointing at the radio. "Life's too short to worry about weather reports."

I flipped off the radio and hoped it poured. We hadn't received rain in a while and it was definitely wanted. In life, Ruby had worried about very little and in death, the things that concerned her totaled out at zero. I, however, fretted about our changing weather patterns, the flowers in my planters that desperately needed rain, and the dryness of the forests and deserts. One spark of lightning could set Sedona and the surrounding areas on fire.

When we arrived at the lawyer's office, I counted two cars in the parking lot.

"Either business isn't booming, or I was right to hustle you out of the house early," Ruby said. "We may be the first ones here."

As we entered the building, I found Penny standing at her desk tossing picture frames and pens into a box. She glanced up at me, and I recalled her pale, puffy face from when Ruby had pointed her out to me as we'd left the murder scene. With her red eyes and even more swollen cheeks, she'd obviously been crying and unfortunately reminded me of a very upset Pillsbury Dough Boy.

She sniffed and dabbed her nose with a tissue. "I'd ask if I could be of help to you, but I don't work here any longer."

Ricky had said his first order of business would be to fire Penny. Apparently, he hadn't wasted any time.

"Ricky!" she yelled over her shoulder. "You've got a client!"

"I'm not expecting anyone," he called. "Please get a name and number."

Penny shook her head and rolled her eyes. "You fired me, Ricky. I'm not doing anything for you." Then she lowered her voice and said, "He's got rocks for brains. I think it's the steroids."

Ruby and I traded glances. Penny tucked the box under her arm and lodged it against her hip.

"Can I help you with that?" I asked, wanting to speak further with the former receptionist.

"No, thank you, sweetie."

"Tell her your grandma always liked her!" Ruby said when the woman strolled toward the front door.

I repeated the words, and Penny turned to me. "Her name was Ruby," I said. "I'm Bernie."

Penny smiled, her fluffy cheeks almost closing her eyes. "I remember Ruby. She was so fun, but a bit obnoxious, no offense to you."

"Oh, I agree," I said truthfully as Ruby shot me a glare. "No offense taken."

"Stanley did a lot of work for her. She was a bit of a personality."

"I'm sorry for your loss," I said. "I understand that you worked for him for many years."

"Thirty. We built this place together. I was his sole employee until he hired the jerk in there."

Tears started cascading down her cheeks again. "I don't know what I'm going to do now. I suppose I'll retire."

"Can I help you?" Ricky said as he rounded the corner. "Penny, don't you have somewhere to be?"

"Oh, this guy deserves a boot in his nether region," Ruby said. "If I were alive, I'd gladly oblige."

Penny had intricate information on the workings of the office—she'd been there for thirty years. Since she'd been fired and was obviously upset, I hoped she'd want to spill *all* the beans. I pivoted away from Ricky, hoping he couldn't hear me. "Can I talk to you, Penny?"

"I suppose so," she said, staring at the man. "Let's go outside though. The air in here suddenly stinks."

"That's fine," I replied, smiling. Ricky would have to wait.

Penny glared at him one more time and gave him the one-finger salute over her shoulder as she marched out the door. With a weak grin, I followed her.

"Good to see Penny's still got a bit of a kick in her," Ruby said. "Too bad she can't lift her leg and kick *him* right in the face."

Penny unlocked her car and set her box in the backseat, then turned to me. "What can I do for you?"

"What can you tell me about Ricky? When did Stanley bring him in?"

She nodded and pursed her lips together. "I believe that history plays an important role in what's happened today. Every moment is connected to the next. Every decision affects the next."

"Penny's getting a bit philosophical," Ruby mused. "Go with it. Let her talk. She loves to talk."

"So, if you don't mind, I'd like to tell you about the beginning," Penny continued, laying her palm on my forearm.

"Of course."

"Let's go to Canyon Coffee," she suggested. "I'm suddenly exhausted."

Canyon Coffee sat right around the corner from the police station. Adam and I used to visit the establishment frequently. Hopefully, he wouldn't decide to drop in while I sat with Penny. "I'll meet you there."

As Ruby and I drove over, she said, "Now remember, Penny rambles. Try to keep her on track with the conversation because if you don't, you'll find yourself listening about the mating habits of the South African monkey or why Pluto is no longer considered a planet. That one's a talker."

I wouldn't mind spending some time discussing Pluto. As far as I was concerned, the little guy had been shortchanged when his title was stripped. Not too many people liked to commiserate with me on that one.

When we were settled in a corner table, me drinking a vanilla latte and Penny having a hot chocolate with whipped cream, she finally got down to our conversation.

"Stanley opened the business thirty years ago and hired me as his secretary. He had no clients, and our office was in his garage. It consisted of two desks, one small file cabinet, and a coffee maker. But slowly, the business grew and he purchased the building it's in now."

I'd been able to situate myself so I could keep an eye on the front door. Every couple of seconds I glanced over to make sure Adam hadn't decided he needed a jolt of caffeine. He wouldn't be happy catching me in a discussion with who I had to assume was one of the murder suspects.

"Stanley and I went through a lot, not only professionally, but personally. I had to turn a blind eye to his affairs. I lied to his wife, Ann. I pretended not to see the charges for dinners and hotels in the surrounding towns over the weekends, especially when I'd run into Ann while Stanley was gone. I remained loyal to the man, even though I didn't like the way he lived his life and treated his wife."

I tried to imagine living and working in that type of environment. *Exhausting* was the word that came to mind.

"In fact, one time I saw Ann in this very place when Stanley said they were going out of town. This was about two years ago. She wore a lovely turquoise necklace that really brought out the blue in her eyes. Don't you find it fascinating how some people's eyes change color based on what they wear? If Ann wears anything blue, her eyes look ethereal. But if she wears green, it brings out the green specks. I find it so interesting."

I nodded and guessed this was where I had to steer the conversation back on track. I mentally tucked the tidbit on the turquoise necklace for further review later. "It must have been difficult to work with Stanley."

"It was, but overall, I liked him, and I did love my job. I found it satisfying to keep the office running and organized. Every day when I left, I felt fulfilled, despite Stanley's dalliances."

"When did he bring in Ricky?" I asked after taking a long sip of my latte.

Penny sniffed and frowned. "Six months ago. Stanley had some health issues and decided he needed the help. I was hesitant, but it's not my office. I tried to make the best of it."

"How did he find Ricky?"

"I'm not sure. There were a couple of other people who came in to interview that I really liked, but Stanley said they weren't a good fit. Then he hired Ricky. That was such a poor choice, and one I'll never understand."

"Why was he a poor choice?"

Penny sighed, took a long sip from her cup, then rolled her eyes. "Have you met the man?"

Briefly, right after finding Stanley. I hadn't liked him then in the least bit, but I'd also been stressed having just discovered a dead body and come face to face with my ex-boyfriend. "I spent a few minutes with him the day Stanley died."

She shook her head. "Stanley didn't *die*. He was *murdered*." She leaned across the table and whispered, "And I'm a suspect."

Arching an eyebrow, I tried to appear surprised, even though the sheriff had found what he alleged to be the murder weapon in Penny's desk drawer: eyedrops. "Really?"

Penny nodded. "They think it was me because I had eyedrops in my desk drawer. I stare at that computer all day long and Stanley had horrible allergies, especially when the sagebrush was in bloom. Of course I kept that stuff handy!" She shook her head and glanced around the café as if she suspected someone was listening. "I didn't kill Stanley. What would be my motive?"

I tried to think of a reason why she'd want her boss of thirty years dead. Maybe she got tired of ignoring his affairs? Perhaps she did it as revenge for Ann? Maybe Stanley had fired her and she'd exacted vengeance, hoping to keep her job after he died and Ricky was in charge? But did the old woman have it in her to do it?

"You better wrap this party up so we can get back to the law office," Ruby said, nearly causing me to jump out of my skin. She'd been so quiet, I'd forgotten she'd accompanied me when I left the house. "She didn't kill anyone."

"Are you okay, Bernie?" Penny asked, her brow furrowed in worry.

"I'm fine," I said. "But I do have to get going. I have some business to discuss with Ricky."

Penny rolled her eyes again and shook

her head. "He's worthless, Bernie. Find another lawyer."

After finishing my coffee, I smiled. "Thanks for your time. I appreciate you talking to me."

"You know, I really did like your grandmother," Penny said. "She was a handful, but a woman with a good heart. We wrote up her will when she decided to leave you the house."

I glanced at my ghost. "I do love living there. I'm very thankful she left it to me."

"She originally had it going to her daughter... your mother. But then she said she wanted it to go to someone who would appreciate it, not just sell it and cash out. She loved you very much."

Ruby's face softened and she grinned. "She's right about that one."

"Thanks again, Penny," I said, standing. "Take care."

Just as Ruby and I approached the door, I glanced up to see Adam standing on the other side.

"Dang it," I whispered under my breath. "I knew this would happen."

CHAPTER 8

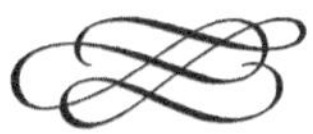

"Bernie!" Adam said. "What are you doing here?"

I stepped aside so he could enter, giving him my friendliest smile. "Just having coffee."

Being the curious cop he was, he glanced at my hands. "Where's your cup?"

"I finished. You know I love the lattes—I suck down their sugary goodness pretty fast. I need to go. Have a great day."

"Hold on a second," he said, grabbing my arm. His gaze darted over the shop patrons and quickly landed on Penny. His touch warmed my arm through my coat. "Were you talking to Penny?"

As I was about to deny knowing her, I glanced over my shoulder at her and she smiled, then waved. "We spoke for a few moments," I said, sighing as his hand fell away.

"What about? Hopefully not Stanley's death."

"Take the offensive position!" Ruby yelled. "Don't let him tackle you like that! Outrun him!"

What the heck did that mean? I glanced at Ruby for a little help.

She rolled her eyes and threw her hands up in the air. "Tell him Penny and I were good friends!"

"Penny knew Ruby," I said, surprised by how smoothly the lie fell from my lips. "She wanted to talk about her a bit."

"Ah. I see." His gaze darted from me to his right then left and his features softened. "Is she here?" he whispered.

"Of course I'm here, copper!" Ruby said sidling up to him. His eyes widened as she laced her arm through his, stood on her tip-toes, and blew in his ear.

"She's right next to me, isn't she? My

arm's cold and I can smell her." I nodded and smiled.

"Seems like the copper's put on a few pounds," Ruby said. "His pants appear a bit tight. He's probably depression-eating over the loss of you."

Adam appeared as fit as ever to me. His blond hair could use a trim, but his blue eyes seemed... ethereal... above his blue turtleneck, just as Penny had pointed out about Stanley's wife, Ann. I realized Adam's eye color also turned depending on what he wore. While in his brown uniform the day I'd found Stanley, his gaze had been blue, but not with the intensity of today.

"Are you okay?" Adam asked.

I was staring. Hard. How embarrassing. "Fine. Everything's fine."

"You two are such star-crossed lovers, you belong on the Love Boat," Ruby quipped, then broke out into the theme song.

"I better get going," I said. "Take care, Adam."

"You as well, Bernie."

Standing in place for a moment, I hoped

to hear him say that he'd been thinking about me again. That he wanted to get back together. That he loved me. That he was at least sorry for throwing me under the bus with the sheriff when I found the body. Instead, he turned and got in line for his coffee.

After pushing open the door, the cool, fresh air took some of the fire out of my cheeks and I inhaled deeply.

"Bernie and the copper sitting in a tree!" Ruby yelled.

"Stop," I hissed.

"K-I-S-S-I-N-G."

"Don't. I mean it. Knock it off."

I glanced up to see a couple coming toward me and by the sheer confusion on their faces, they'd witnessed me speaking to the air. I waited for them to pass, then turned to Ruby. "He doesn't care about me anymore, so cool it."

"Don't be so dense," she moaned, rolling her eyes. "Of course he does. He's playing hard to get. Where are we headed now?"

"Back to the lawyer's office," I replied. Even though I was on the hunt for a killer, I still did have to find a way to lower my taxes.

"WHAT DO YOU WANT?' Ricky asked, his voice dripping with exasperation. When he crossed his arms over his chest, his shirt pulled at the seams and I wondered if he bought his clothing too small to make his muscles appear larger. His glare held shades of confusion. He probably recognized me but wasn't sure from where. We stood in the front office and I noted he'd already re-arranged Penny's desk and the reception chairs. That hadn't taken long.

"I'm looking for someone to help me with some business restructuring," I said. "We met the day Stanley... died. And a while ago I left here with Penny."

Did he know Stanley's death was considered a murder?

"That's right," he said, snapping his fingers. "I thought I recognized you. I don't do that type of work anymore. Sorry." He turned and hurried back into his office.

"Follow him," Ruby urged. "Let's go."

Having been ceremoniously dismissed, anger heated my cheeks. I walked the fine line of standing up for myself and becoming an irritation to Ricky. If I bothered him enough, he'd either help me or become even more annoyed.

"One foot in front of the other," Ruby said, waving me forward. "Hurry up. What do you have to lose? Hearing him tell you no once again? Big deal!"

But what did I have to gain? I hoped for some help with my business and maybe some other secret information Ruby and I could gather.

Before I could give it anymore thought, I hurried into his office. Boxes had been piled up against the wall as if he were packing. "Are you going somewhere?" I asked.

"I'm moving into Stanley's old office in back," he grumbled. "More room."

He muttered something about me minding my own business, but I ignored the comment. "Look, I need some help," I said as Ruby rounded the desk and stood behind him. "Stanley was going to restructure my business. Why can't you do that for me?"

A minor lie, but I didn't see the harm. Having never spoken to Stanley, I could only *assume* he would've assisted me with the paperwork.

"Because I'm a criminal lawyer," Ricky said, sighing as he glared at me. I'd obviously irritated him.

"I've been told many times that Stanley did paperwork like this," I insisted. "Now he's gone. Why aren't you stepping in to take his place?"

Ruby was almost on top of Ricky, looking over his shoulder at the file open in front of him. I kept my distance so he wouldn't feel the need to close it and Ruby could keep reading.

"Look, lady. I'm not doing that type of law any longer, okay?"

"Keep talking!" Ruby said as she bent over to study his computer.

Ricky sneezed and he reached for a tissue to blow his nose. "I'm going to have to ask you to leave. I have a client coming in at any moment and I need to be prepared for my meeting. You aren't helping me."

Crossing my arms over my chest, I gave him my best I'm-not-happy glare. "If you aren't going to assist me, where would you suggest I go?"

Ruby moved in closer, her face now right next to his as she squinted at the screen. Ricky sneezed again and his eyes began to water. "Are you wearing lavender perfume or lotion?" he asked.

I smiled and shook my head. "Why?"

"I smell lavender and I'm allergic to it."

As his eyes swelled, I bit my lip to keep from laughing.

With a mischievous grin, Ruby yelled, "Boo!" right in his face, sending off another round of sneezing.

"You'll have to excuse me," he said, standing. "I need to find some allergy pills." As he brushed by me, he yelled, "Penny!"

"She doesn't work here anymore!" I called. "You fired her, remember?"

While he sputtered and coughed, Ruby cackled and tried to chase after him—but once she arrived at the end of our tether, she snapped back into range.

"Come on!" she shouted. "I want to go make him sneeze more!"

I shook my head. "Let's not torture the poor guy any further, okay?" I whispered.

"But he deserves it!" Ruby whined. "He probably killed Stanley!"

Ricky let out at least a dozen sneezes in the hallway—I lost count after eight—while I snuck behind his desk to take a glance at what he'd been working on. It had nothing to do with any case, but it did prove to be an interesting discovery.

Ruby and I had been wrong on what would happen to the office. According to the papers in the file, Stanley's wife, Ann, had had no holdings in the law business. Since Ricky was partner and the way the business was structured, everything went to him. I did note that Stanley owned the building outright so I imagined Ann would have Ricky pay rent. At least she'd get something out of the deal. Or perhaps she'd just sell the place and leave Ricky to fend for himself. No matter which way it was diced,

Ricky may be the most unlikeable person I'd associated with this case so far.

A string of curses filtered in from the hallway. Poor Ricky's reaction to lavender seemed to be getting worse, and I grinned.

"Uh oh," Ruby said.

I glanced up to see a hulking man in the doorway—even bigger than Ricky.

"That's Gunner," Ruby said. "The guy Jezzy used to date and maybe still does. Their relationship was always on-again, off-again."

I stared up at the bald Black man with the thick black beard. His muscles bulged under his tattoos as he shoved his hands into the front pockets of his jeans. He wore a white t-shirt under his Moonlit Coffin cut. "Where's Ricky?" he asked, his voice deep—almost a growl.

"He's having an allergy attack out there," I said, my voice just above a whisper while I pointed behind him. The small office seemed to be shrinking with every moment. Even if I wanted to run out of the building, I wouldn't be able to get past the hulking man.

"Who're you?"

I cleared my throat. "My name's Bernie. I was hoping to hire Ricky, but it doesn't look like he's going to take my case."

"What did you do?"

"It's... it's just paperwork," I said. "If you'll excuse me."

As he stepped aside, I slid past him. The top of my head came up to his mid-chest and his stare followed me until I was out the door.

Would he tell Ricky he'd found me behind his desk?

"Wait a minute!" Ruby shouted. "Hold up!"

Turning back to the office, I noticed Ricky and Gunner walk down the hall toward Stanley's old office.

"Come on!" Ruby said. "We need to go back inside!"

Without giving it much thought, I followed her in and gently closed the door. I felt exposed standing in the middle of the room, so I crouched down behind Penny's desk. Ruby stood right next to me. Anyone looking in from the front would see me, but if Ricky and Gunner came out from the back, they wouldn't, and that's all the mattered.

"It looks like you're getting settled here," Gunner growled. His voice held a hint of danger and caused a chill to travel over my arms. If I was caught, those arms could snap me right in half.

"Yes. I fired Penny this morning, so I think everything will work out the way I want."

"We did what you asked us to," Gunner said. "So make sure the case is taken care of, okay?"

"Of course. Everything will go fine."

We did what you asked us to. Had I just heard an admission of murder?

"Let's get out of here," I said under my breath. I quickly crawled across the carpet and pushed open the door. Glancing over my shoulder, I thankfully found the hallway empty. I stood and hurried out to my car, where I pulled out my keys with trembling fingers. We drove out of the parking lot, and only then did I take a few deep breaths.

Once calm, I considered what I'd

learned. With Stanley's death, Ricky was now owner of the law firm. He answered to no one.

He'd gotten exactly what he wanted.

And it sounded like Gunner from Moonlit Coffin could have been the killer.

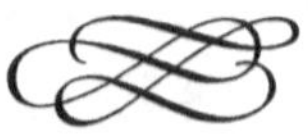

RUBY HUMMED next to me as I sped home. "Why are you so calm?" I yelled. "We just heard a man admit to committing murder!"

"If you're talking about Gunner, we did not," she said, shaking her head. "And although I love speed, you're going to get yourself a ticket if you keep this up."

Glancing down at the speedometer, I realized I was going sixty in a thirty mile per hour speed zone. I eased off the accelerator and checked my rearview mirror for the hundredth time in the past two minutes. No one followed me.

"You better practice those breathing exercises for stress you like so much before you give yourself a heart attack," Ruby muttered, glancing over at me. "You're wound up tighter than a too-small pair of knickers on a fat bottom."

She wasn't wrong. As I took some deep breaths, I also lessened my death-grip on the steering wheel.

"There you go," she said. "Good girl."

As we pulled into the lot behind my house, I felt a little calmer. However, I knew what I'd heard and it had definitely sounded as if Gunner had done Ricky's dirty work. I turned to Ruby and she held her hand up. "Don't start talking yet. Let's go inside so I can see Elvira."

I sighed with frustration, needing to re-hash what we'd heard. How in the world could my ghost be so cool and collected?

After yanking off my coat and hanging it up, I grabbed a cup of water and heated it in the microwave, then dumped in a chamomile tea bag. The British would be horrified at my actions, but I didn't possess a kettle or the patience to wait for the water to boil. I went into the living room and found

Ruby and my disloyal cat curled up on the couch together.

"Are you feeling better?" Ruby asked.

I nodded and sat down. "Do you think they knew I was in the office?"

"Of course not," she replied, shaking her head. "They would've come after you if they did."

After taking a long sip of tea, I leaned my head back against the cushions. It had been foolish to return to the office after I'd met Gunner, but *foolish* seemed to be my middle name when I was with Ruby.

"I'd be surprised if Gunner had anything to do with Stanley's death," Ruby continued. "Even if it sounded like he did."

"That was a confession if I'd ever heard one."

"You don't know that. Maybe Ricky has a motorcycle and Moonlit Coffin helped him with repairs. It could be something as simple as that."

"What about Ricky?"

"That guy's guiltier than a skunk is stinky," Ruby said, moving her ghostly hand over my purring cat. "That's who we concentrate on. It's the perfect set up. He wanted to bring in the criminal element into the office and Stanley didn't. Ricky becomes partner and realizes he can have the whole office to himself and do what he pleases. He killed Stanley with Penny's eyedrops."

An incredibly solid theory. Yet, what Gunner had said really stuck with me. Ruby was certain of his innocence, but I found it hard to believe that the golf-shirt wearing, clean cut lawyer could pull off a murder. A tattooed leather-clad member of a biker gang seemed more up for the job. However, I did have a horrible habit of judging people by their looks...

I had no idea what my next move should be. "We need to go to Adam."

"Not yet," Ruby said, standing. "Right now, you need to change into your workout clothes and go see Jezebel. You have class soon."

"I completely forgot," I grumbled. "I don't want to go."

Thankfully, my self-defense skills had improved, but that only meant Jezebel challenged me more with the reasoning that she was trying to expand my abilities. Most of it felt like she was trying to dislodge a rib.

"Go on, now. Quit whining, finish up your tea, and let's go to Tip 'Em Back."

With a curse, I did as instructed.

"HEY, BERNIE!" Jezebel called from behind the bar as Ruby and I walked in. It took a few moments for my eyes to adjust until I could see her. Today her long, blonde hair cascaded around her toned and tattooed shoulders. She grinned as she wiped out a glass behind the old wooden bar. "Ruby, you're not as bad as people said you were. In fact, you're worse."

Jezebel didn't bother to ask if my ghost was with me any longer because she knew Ruby would never let me come to Tip 'Em Back on my own. It had been her chosen hangout spot while alive and Jezebel had been one of her favorite people. To greet each other, they always exchanged insults.

Ruby snickered. "Jezzy, I don't think

you're dumb. You just have bad luck when it comes to thinking."

I relayed the message and the three of us burst out into peals of laughter.

On the wall to my right hung decades of pictures including ones of Jezebel and her grandmother, Janis, who passed away before Ruby. I stared at the picture of Ruby and me when I was younger and came to visit her during the summers. I wished I could remember ever being at the bar back then, but I always drew a blank.

Ruby pointed at me. "Ask Jezzy if she's still Gunner's old lady. When she saw him last. Stuff like that."

I considered Jezebel my friend, but I still walked on eggshells when around her at times. Or maybe it was just me being uncomfortable with myself because she'd never been anything but kind to me. Except when she was tossing me around, but even then it wasn't malicious. In a nutshell, she scared me a bit. Physically strong and a former fighter, she could probably break every bone in my body with one hand tied behind her back.

"Ruby wants to know if you're still seeing Gunner," I asked.

Jezebel set down the glass and picked up another. "Yeah, we're back together," she replied, sighing. "Can't seem to get rid of him, no matter how hard I try."

"It's called love," Ruby said. "Just like you can't get over Adam."

Ugh. I hated that.

"Go ahead, tell her what you heard," Ruby urged. I stood silently unsure how to bring up the fact I thought her boyfriend was a murderer. "See what she's got to say. It's not like she's going to throw a glass at you or jump over the bar and beat your face in."

She might when I accuse her boyfriend of killing someone.

"What's up, Bernie?" Jezebel asked. "You're staring at me like you want to say something but you can't find the words. I don't bite. Well, not that hard, anyway, so spill it."

I sighed and crossed my arms over my chest. "Did you hear about the death of the lawyer?"

"Oh, yeah. Broke my brittle heart. Stanley was my grandmother's lawyer and he took care of a couple items for me. Good guy."

"He was murdered."

Jezebel arched an eyebrow as she wiped down the glass. "I hadn't heard that part. Only that he was dead. How do you know? Pillow talk with Adam?"

"No," I replied, shaking my head. "I found the body. Adam and I hadn't seen each other in weeks until then."

As she narrowed her gaze and stared at me for a long moment, I figured she was trying to gauge how believable my story was. Finally, she said, "That should surprise me, but it doesn't. Why do you think he was murdered?"

"The sheriff speculated on it that day and Stanley's lips were blue, which I unfortunately know can mean poisoning. They found eyedrops in the secretary's desk, so they were thinking that's the murder weapon. Penny, the secretary, told me she was a suspect."

"What does any of this have to do with

me?" she asked, setting down the glass and towel. I had her full attention.

"Let's say I was somewhere I wasn't supposed to be. I heard... I heard Gunner and Stanley's partner, Ricky, talking. Gunner said some things that made me think he could be involved in the murder."

She didn't confirm or deny it. Instead, she stared at me stone-faced. "Where were you when you overheard Gunner say these damaging things? And how do you know him?"

"I was at the lawyer's office. We'd met briefly before this incident and Ruby told me who he was."

"When did this happen?"

"Earlier today."

"And Gunner and Ricky didn't know you were there?"

I shook my head.

"And was Ruby with you?"

"Yes."

Jezebel bit her lip and glanced around the bar. Finally, her stare settled back on me. "I think you better stop playing cops and robbers, Bernie. You're going to find yourself in a heap of trouble."

A chill traveled down my spine as bile rose in my throat. Was my friend looking out for me, or had I just been threatened?

Time to change the subject. "Have you had any dealings with Ricky?"

Jezebel shook her head. "But I've heard he's playing on a field he doesn't belong."

"Ask her if the coppers have spoken to Gunner," Ruby said.

I repeated the question. "Not that I know of," Jezebel replied. "But the police are always sniffing around Moonlit Coffin, so it wouldn't be anything new or a hot topic of conversation."

Why didn't I know this? I'd dated Adam for months and I was just now finding out he investigated Moonlit Coffin on a regular basis? I'd thought we'd had an open and honest relationship and he never once mentioned the biker gang. Perhaps because it was confidential police information? Even then, it still hurt. What else hadn't he shared with me?

"What do you want from me, Bernie?"

Jezebel asked. "Why are you telling me all this?"

"I was hoping you could introduce me to Gunner."

She furrowed her brow, confusion darkening her blue gaze. "Why?"

"I wanted to talk to him about Stanley's murder."

And there it was. I'd painted myself into a corner by being honest with Jezebel. I'd basically accused her boyfriend of killing someone, and now I'd just requested an introduction so I could ask him questions about it.

"You aren't very good at this stuff," Ruby mumbled next to me. "Why in the heck is she going to get you access to Gunner when you're trying to prove he killed Stanley?"

Jezebel sighed and shook her head. "Bernie, you're wading into some pretty murky waters here."

"I just want to talk to him," I said. "That's all. Is he going to be here tonight? Ruby said Moonlit Coffin likes to hang out at the bar."

"Yeah, he'll be around tonight," she replied, picking up another glass and the towel. "I can introduce you, but tread carefully, Bernie. I say that because I like you and consider you a friend. You have no idea what you're getting yourself into. Okay?"

And for the third time, my friend had warned me away from talking to her boyfriend.

"Do you still want to work out today, or are you too busy playing Nancy Drew?" Jezebel asked.

"It's Starsky and Hutch to you, sweetheart," Ruby said. "Or Riggs and Murtaugh. Oh! I know! Cagney and Lacey!"

Ignoring Ruby, I said, "Yes. I want to."

Jezebel set down the glass and towel once more. "Let's head on back."

As I followed Jezebel to the back room, I laid my hand over my thundering heart as beads of sweat dotted my brow and nervous butterflies tickled my belly. But this time, it wasn't the idea of Jezebel tossing me around that had my system in an uproar. It was what she'd said about me staying away from Gunner. She didn't want me speaking to him, which led me to the question: Had I discovered the killer?

CHAPTER 10

I SAT on my bed in my empty house trying not to listen to all the creaks and moans as the wind blew outside, my nightstand lamp the only light illuminating the room. Running my hand over the yellow comforter, I picked up my phone and glanced at the clock. It was finally time to leave.

Hurrying into the bathroom, I checked my reflection one last time. My black hair swirled around my shoulders and I'd applied a little eyeliner and blush, along with mascara. Ruby had insisted I wear a black turtleneck instead of my *Moonstruck* T-shirt so I'd fit in a little better. Apparently, bikers didn't appreciate the finer movies.

"Let's go! Let's go!" she said, appearing behind me. "I haven't been this excited since the debut of *The Mary Tyler Moore Show*. Hurry up!"

"What about the birth of your daughter?"

"Okay, that was a happy time."

"What about *my* birth?"

"Jeez, Bernie!" she yelled, throwing her hands up in the air. "Fine! There were a few other things that were slightly more important than the TV show! Can we please go now?"

I snickered and winked. "Love you, Ruby."

"Shut up and get your tush in gear," she said, smiling. "I love you, too."

With each mile we drove, my palms sweated a little more and my stomach flipped. Once again, I was walking directly into a situation that not only made me extremely uncomfortable, but could also be potentially dangerous. I could only hope that my relationship with Jezebel protected me from any ill-intentions Moonlit Coffin may have when I started asking questions.

"There are so many people here," I said as we pulled into the dirt parking lot. I noticed a few bikes lined up by the front door, but the sheer number of cars astounded me.

"Tip 'Em Back is the best place to be any night of the week," Ruby replied. "And if you weren't such a homebody, we could've come here before now."

"I'm tired," I grumbled. "I work a lot."

"That may be part of the problem," Ruby muttered as I parked in a space close to the street. "Let's go have some fun!"

Questioning a biker gang about murder didn't fall into any realm of fun I could fathom.

Taking some deep breaths, I slipped out of the car and jammed the keys into my coat. I'd opted to leave my purse at home—one less thing to keep track of. The jukebox blared seventies rock n' roll, the music loud and clear through the closed doors.

"Oh! I can't wait to dance!" Ruby squealed as she ghosted inside. Laying my palm on the handle, I tried to find my bravery. A second later, Ruby came back to my side. "Come on! What are you waiting for? The second coming of Jesus?"

I pulled open the door. The odor of beer, stale cigarettes from years gone by, and bodies slammed into me like a fist. Glancing around, I found a packed house. Men and women filled all the tables and laughter wafted through the air. In the corner, a group played darts. Others danced by the jukebox. Overall, everyone seemed to be having a good time.

Weaving my way through the crowd toward the bar, I found Jezebel laughing as she poured beers and served her customers. Once a place cleared, I moved in to speak with her.

"Hey, Bernie!" she yelled over the music. "Welcome! You want a beer?"

I nodded and pulled out a ten-dollar bill. Once she set the frothy mug in front of me, she pushed the money back at me. "On the house," she mouthed with a wink.

"Thanks," I yelled. "You're sure busy!"

"On Wednesdays things start to pick up because it's hump day and everyone's ready to pretend it's Friday."

As I glanced around the bar again, I noted Ruby dancing a few feet away, her hands up in the air and hips swaying, her smile as bright as the sun. "I love this!" she shouted. "I feel like my heart's beating again!"

A headache began to form behind my eyes. Was I a party pooper or just unaccustomed to being up so late?

"They're over there!" Jezebel pointed toward the front door. After a moment, I found Gunner sitting at a table with another hulking man. I'd walked right by them on my way in.

Grabbing my beer, I headed over. The temptation to stride right past them and out the front door was strong. Gunner eyed me warily while the other man motioned for me to sit down. Each had a small shot glass in front of them filled with amber liquid, as well as a full beer bottle.

I eyed the new guy as I lowered myself into the chair. Tall and not quite as broad in the shoulders as Gunner, his piercing blue gaze never left me. He ran a hand through his long blond hair. "I understand you wanted to speak with us." His hard, gruff voice twisted my stomach further. I was so out of my comfort zone, I may as well have been on another planet.

"They smell your fear," Ruby said, leaning down so her head was right next to mine, "Heck, I smell your fear and I'm dead. You better give off some brave vibes."

"My name's Bernie," I said, staring at the newcomer. "And you are?"

"Thunder. I'm the head honcho of Moonlit Coffin."

Recalling Darla saying he liked BLTs and vanilla milkshakes, I smiled and took a sip of my beer. Maybe this wouldn't be so bad after all. How dangerous could a guy who liked vanilla milkshakes be? "It's nice to meet you." Sliding my gaze over to Gunner, I said, "We met briefly."

He nodded and smiled. "I recall. It's hard to forget a pretty face like yours."

"Oh, what a charmer!" Ruby exclaimed. "Not only is he cute in a rugged, outlaw way, but a smooth talker. I always liked him. Can't hold his tequila too well, though."

Gunner's dark gaze glittered with happiness or amusement—I wasn't sure which—and it definitely made him seem less harmless than Thunder and his dead-eyed stare.

"What can we do for you?" Thunder asked.

Technically, I'd only wanted to talk to Gunner, which had been nerve-wracking enough. Add in Thunder and I fought the urge to toss my cookies all over the table. But I had to move forward.

"I wanted to speak to Gunner about the death of Stanley Jones. The lawyer."

"What about it?" Thunder asked.

My gaze darted from Gunner to Thunder. Why wasn't Gunner speaking?

"Well, I was wondering where he was that afternoon."

Thunder narrowed his stare. "The afternoon the lawyer died? Why?"

Gunner leaned forward and placed his elbows on the table. "He didn't just die. He was killed, right?"

I nodded.

"And you think Gunner has something to do with it?" Thunder asked.

"Not specifically," I lied as I swallowed

the bile rising in my throat. My fight or flight defenses had gone into overdrive and the impulse to flee became almost overwhelming.

"Let me tell you something, little lady," Thunder said, his nostrils flared as he pointed at me. "I don't know who you think you are, but if you go around accusing people of murder, you're going to find yourself—"

Another threat. Wonderful.

"It's okay," Gunner said, smiling as he laid a hand over Thunder's finger. "I've got nothing to hide."

I took another sip of my beer hoping my shaky hands weren't too obvious.

"On that afternoon, I was with Jezebel," he said. "She can verify that for me."

"Well, well, well. Isn't that convenient?" Ruby mused. "Maybe I was wrong about Gunner. Maybe he did have something to do with it."

My thoughts exactly.

"Stanley's partner, Ricky, is handling a case for us," he continued.

"We don't need to go into that," Thunder

growled, his hard gaze still on me. "Why are we bothering to talk to her anyway? It's not like she's a cop or something."

"Because Jezebel asked us to," Gunner said. "There's no harm in talking to the pretty lady."

Placing my hands in my lap, I laced my fingers together to hide my trembling. "There's speculation that Moonlit Coffin had something to do with Stanley's death," I said. "I'm just trying to find the truth."

"But why?" Thunder asked. "You're not a cop. Why do you care?"

"Tell him you do freelance writing for the paper," Ruby urged. "That sounds better than you're gathering evidence for the police and you know a gang of bikers is more likely to talk to you than a copper."

"I write for the paper," I said. "I'm trying to get a good story."

"Jezebel never mentioned that," Gunner said.

"I never told her," I replied, shrugging.

To my utter astonishment, Thunder seemed to buy it. "As President of Moonlit Coffin, I will say we don't like to be featured in the papers unless it's for our charity work. You ever hear of our Ride for Life?"

I shook my head.

"We ride with a blood bank truck and escort them to the local communities and urge people to give blood. We would rather gather blood and help those in need than spill it. Why don't you print that?"

"Yeah, that should've made the papers," Ruby muttered. "That's a good thing."

Glancing over at Gunner, I found him staring back at me with a grin as he crossed his arms over his chest. I may have Thunder believing my story, but I had doubts Gunner did.

"I'll ask someone about it," I replied. "But I'm still interested in what Moonlit Coffin's relationship was with Stanley and his partner, Ricky Summers."

"Ricky does some work for us," Thunder said. "Stanley didn't exist, as far as I'm concerned."

Interesting choice of words.

"Why do you say that?" I asked.

"Because I had no reason to speak to the man."

"And what about you?" I asked, gazing directly at Gunner. I sounded much braver than I felt. "Did you and Stanley have dealings?"

He shook his head. "Nothing."

I didn't know what I was expecting, but I'd apparently reached a dead end. No one wanted to share information with me, but I knew what I'd heard Gunner say to Ricky: *We did what you asked us to.*

But as it had been pointed out, that could mean anything from mailing a letter to murder.

"How're things going over here?" Jezebel asked, placing her hand on my shoulder and giving it a squeeze. "Everyone okay? Can I get you anything?"

I grabbed my beer and slammed down the remnants. Not being a big beer drinker, I immediately belched. *Classy.* For good measure, my stomach rolled and heaved. Between the alcohol and my nerves, I was in for a doozy of a night with gastrointestinal issues. "I'm fine."

Thunder smiled up at Jezebel. "We're

done with her, but Gunner and I will have another shot."

They both picked up their glasses and slammed them down, then looked up at Jezebel expectantly.

"I'm on it," she said, returning to the bar.

"Can I walk you out to your car?" Gunner asked, standing.

"No! We aren't ready to go!" Ruby wailed, but the way Gunner eyed me, I felt like I had no choice but to leave.

I nodded, both scared to death to be alone with him and oddly curious. He wouldn't hurt me because of my relationship with his girlfriend. Well, that's what I hoped. But why offer to walk me to my car?

The wind still howled as we stepped outside, Ruby grumbling next to me.

"Where are you parked?" he asked.

I pointed to the back of the lot.

We walked in silence, threading between the vehicles until we reached my car. After using the key fob to unlock the door, I opened it, but Gunner placed his big hand on the window and shut it. I gasped as he moved in closer to me, trapping me be-tween his big body and my vehicle.

"Shoot for the family jewels!" Ruby screamed. "Make him sing soprano! What kind of monster is he? How did I not see this before?"

As I brought my knee up, he blocked it with his leg. "I'm not going to hurt you," he said, his whisky-laced breath caressing my cheek. "I want you to listen very closely to me."

I trembled from head-to-toe as I met his gaze and tears tracked down my cheeks. Coming to talk to Moonlit Coffin had been such a horrible idea.

"Please don't cry," he said. "Take some deep breaths. Let go of your fear for a minute and listen."

I inhaled the cold air and tried not to vomit.

"You need to stay far away from Moonlit Coffin," he said. "I know you're not a jour-nalist. You own a bed and breakfast. You don't grasp who you're messing with. Stay. Away. You *will* get hurt. Do you understand?"

I nodded and he stepped aside.

"Have a good night, Bernie."

As he strolled back to the bar, I leaned over and placed my hands on my knees, exhuming the beer and my dinner onto the dirt.

"That was definitely a threat," Ruby muttered.

It most certainly was, and to me, it only solidified in my mind that Moonlit Coffin was responsible for Stanley's death.

CHAPTER 11

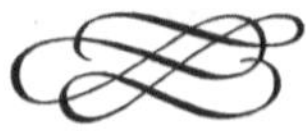

AFTER A NIGHT OF RESTLESS SLEEP, more trips to the bathroom than I could count, and a busy brain that wouldn't quiet down, I woke in a foul mood. Grateful I had no guests, I shuffled into the kitchen to make coffee then sat down at the island while it brewed.

Gunner had been trying to frighten me and it worked for a while. But somewhere in the middle of the night, that fear had turned to anger. I replayed the conversation with both him and Thunder countless times and thought of all the things I should have said. Snappy comebacks. Intelligent questions. A well-placed fist to the nose. And when I re-called the way I had reacted—trembling and vomiting—I became more furious.

"You okay, Bernie?" Ruby asked as I poured myself a cup of coffee.

"Yes," I muttered. "I wish I had donuts."

"Well, that's a sure sign you aren't okay, but—"

I held out my hand in front of me. "Can you please stop talking? My mood is awful and I'm afraid I'm going to say something I'll regret."

Ruby made a zipping gesture across her lips, then tossed her imaginary key over her shoulder. I settled back into my chair with my coffee and hoped the magic elixir would improve my disposition.

As I scrolled through the local news on my phone, I quickly realized I wasn't re-taining anything I read. Setting down the device, I shut my eyes and laid my head on the countertop. Perhaps going back to bed was the answer.

Ruby cleared her throat behind me. "I know you told me to keep my mouth shut, but did you see that Stanley's viewing and funeral is today?"

I sat up and turned around. "What?"

"Sorry, but I was reading over your shoulder. Stanley's funeral is today. We should go. On a lot of TV shows the killer shows up at the funeral."

My first reaction was *absolutely not*, but then I remembered how angry I'd been about the previous night. How dare they threaten me? The investigation started out as a harebrained scheme of Ruby's to get Adam and me back together, but now it had become more. I didn't like being pushed around, and I'd work to solve this case just so I wouldn't back down from Moonlit Coffin. That stunt last night had practically been an admission of guilt.

"Do you have something to wear?" Ruby asked.

At one time I had owned a black pencil skirt. I could pair it with the black turtleneck from last night.

I hurried into my room and opened my closet door. After rummaging through the hanging clothes, I couldn't find the skirt. Maybe I had put it in my donation bag?

Dropping to my knees, I pulled out the garbage bag that had been sitting in my closet for at least a year and dumped everything on the floor. Shoes, an old purse, and clothes fell out. I pawed through them and smiled at my victory. "Found it!" I yelled triumphantly.

"Good!" Ruby said from the bed. "Slip it on and let's see how it looks. What are you going to wear on top?"

"I was thinking the turtleneck from last night."

"You'll need to throw it in the dryer or something. It most likely smells like beer and fear."

She had a point.

I slipped on the skirt, mortified it was so tight. Even without a zipper, it pulled at my hips. "I can't wear this," I said, vowing to get my act together and quit the sweet treats I never used to eat. "It's going to rip at the seams."

"Sure you can. It's only for an hour or

two. You'll be fine. Do you have any of those shapewear tights? That'll help a little."

I scrounged through my drawer and found a pair. Once I was fully dressed, I turned to Ruby.

"What do you think?"

"I think you look very appropriate for a funeral."

AN HOUR later I strode up the walkway to the Gone, but not Forgotten Funeral Home with Ruby in tow.

"Ugh," she said. "I hate funerals. So dang depressing."

I smiled at a few other attendees as I entered and waited to sign the guest book. Even though I'd arrived a bit early, quite a few people mingled about.

"Isn't that dumb?" Ruby asked as I picked up the pen. "He's dead. He doesn't care who came to his funeral."

When I was about to argue that funerals were for the living, not the dead, she gasped, pointed to my left and yelled, "Oh, my word!"

I turned and glanced into the room to find Stanley lying in state, his casket open, surrounded by white roses.

"Why do they do that to people?!" Ruby shouted. "Anyone can see he looks awful! This is the way people are going to remember him! He was ugly in real life and it's worse in death!" She shook her head and placed her hands on her hips. "I'm so glad I didn't do this when I died. Burn me to dust instead of this atrocity."

I wouldn't argue. Even from a distance, I noticed he'd been heavily made up. Keeping my eye on him, I walked into the room and slid into an aisle chair. The more distance between me and Stanley, the happier I was. Besides, the seat offered a great view of everyone in attendance.

"We've got to go pay our respects," Ruby said.

"I'll sit right here," I whispered, having no intention of going near Stanley.

"No, you have to go up there," she insisted. "That's Ann standing next to the casket. She's got her eye on you and you aren't getting out of this one."

I glanced up to find an elderly woman dressed in a black pantsuit staring at me. Rail thin, she stood next to the casket with her hands clasped in front of her looking like she'd rather be tortured than at the funeral. She stood next to another woman, who, judging by their similar features, was somehow related. Smiling, I approached her and she glanced around the room as if she wanted to run.

"Please don't," she said. "I can't take it."

"I'm sorry?"

"Don't tell me how sorry you are for my loss when you've been in Stanley's bed."

Ruby burst out laughing as I stared at the woman, completely speechless.

"She thinks you're one of Stanley's harlots!" Ruby said.

"M-my name's Bernie," I stuttered, determined not to look at the dead man. "Stanley was doing some work for me and I've never... been in... his bed." Just saying the words left a bad taste in my mouth.

Her eyes widened and her cheeks

flushed. "I'm so sorry," she whispered, bringing her hand up to her mouth. "My husband... he was a wanderer. I assumed... I shouldn't have assumed anything."

The woman I thought to be related placed her arm around Ann. "Relax, honey. Just another hour or two."

"It's okay," I soothed, laying my hand on Ann's forearm. "It's a difficult time for you. I wanted to say that Stanley was a good man." I really had no idea, but I'd take Ruby's word.

"Thank you," Ann said as tears welled in her eyes. "I only wish... well, thank you."

"We appreciate your understanding," the other woman said. "I'm Eleanor, Ann's sister."

"It's nice to meet you both." With that, I returned to my seat, relieved to be free of the uncomfortable situation.

With a sigh, I noted those in attendance. Ricky sat a few chairs away from Merry, the owner of Joyous Jewels. She wore her blonde hair up in a bun, her face streaked with tears, making no attempt to hide her grief despite Ann's presence. Ricky's hooded lids indicated he'd most likely be asleep before long. Penny had taken a chair on the other side of the room. No tears for her, but the sadness radiated from her in waves. I tried to catch her eye, but she stared at Stanley as if she was willing him back to life.

A large hand landed on my shoulder and I turned to find Gunner smiling at me. "Nice to see you again," he whispered. "I hope you gave some thought to our chat last night."

He didn't wait for an answer, but instead joined Thunder against the back wall while my heart hammered and my breath caught in my throat. Gunner kept his gaze on me, but Thunder either hadn't noticed me or he'd decided I wasn't worth a greeting.

"The whole cast of characters is here," Ruby said. "Just like on the TV shows. All the suspects have gathered."

A man dressed in a black suit stepped up to a podium I hadn't previously noticed and cleared his throat into the microphone. "If we could all take our seats, we'll get started with the service."

His smooth, droning voice quickly lulled me into a place where I was alone with my own thoughts. Was I sitting in a room with a murderer? Did the killer actually have the audacity to show up at his or her victim's funeral? Were they gloating, thrilled that they'd so far gone undetected, or did they hold a sliver of remorse?

After the service, I was going to head straight home but decided to use the restroom before leaving. As I fought my skirt, I once again vowed to lose the weight I'd gained. My ghost had been a bad influence on my healthy, regimented lifestyle and I needed to make some changes. I used to run almost every day. I'd never consider a pastry at Canyon Coffee or a peanut butter and chocolate delicacy at Sarah's Smoothies. I used to be able look at Darla's food without slobbering all over myself. Yet, the thought of giving any of it up brought a heaviness to my heart because frankly, the little slices of decadence brought me pleasure. Perhaps I had to find a happy medium—a way to enjoy the things I liked every now and then but remain thin and keep my healthy habits most of the time.

Just as I was finishing up, the bathroom door opened.

"I'm so glad that's over!" Ann said. "All the drivel and lies... I couldn't take it anymore."

The sink turned on and I peeked through the slit in my stall. Ruby stood next to the sisters, staring at them silently instead of her usual antics of blowing in people's faces or walking through them to give them a chill. "I know what you mean," her sister, Eleanor, said. "It's a little thick in there."

"Do you think any of those people liked Stanley?" Ann asked as she washed her hands. "Were any of them sincere?"

Eleanor leaned up against the sink away from the mirror and crossed her slim arms over her chest. "I don't know. None of it matters now."

I didn't dare to breathe. They obviously had no idea I was in the stall.

"It doesn't," Ann said, sighing. She turned and grabbed a paper towel. After wetting it, she dabbed her face. "I have to decide what to do about Ricky. Do I let him stay in the building or do I sell it?"

"Do you want to deal with him?"

"Not particularly," Ann replied. "I don't want to deal with any of it."

"I'm here to help you," Eleanor said. "I'll do whatever you need. You can lean on me."

"Yes. I know."

The two sisters embraced and then checked their reflections in the mirror.

"Do you smell lavender?" Eleanor asked as she patted her curls.

"I do. I believe I also smell marijuana. It must be coming in through the ventilation system. I'd smoke it as well if I had to work in a funeral home. Such a depressing place."

"Agreed."

"Agreed," Ruby chimed in. "I'd rather be in jail than in this place."

Ann turned to her sister. "It's probably bad luck for me to speak ill of the dead, especially when he's not even in the ground yet, but I'm glad the jerk's gone."

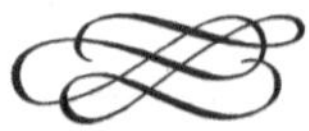

I REMAINED in the bathroom stall a good fifteen minutes after Ann and Eleanor exited.

"You can come out," Ruby said. "I'm sure they're gone."

"I want to be certain," I whispered. "I'd prefer to leave when the building is empty." Another tangle with Moonlit Coffin wouldn't do me any good, either.

As I sat on the closed toilet, I replayed the overheard conversation in my head. Ann obviously was happy Stanley was dead. But had she murdered him? Certainly, she had access to Penny's eyedrops. No one would think it strange for a wife to visit her husband at his place of business. Had his philandering pushed her over the edge and she'd snuck the eyedrops into his coffee?

"I never suspected Ann of offing Stanley, but it makes sense," Ruby mused. "She had motive and opportunity."

I nodded and stood. With a deep breath, I opened the door and washed my hands, then hurried out into the hall. As I passed the now-empty room that held Stanley's body, I noted they'd closed the casket.

"Thank goodness," Ruby muttered. "I'll never be able to unsee the poor man in that state. Awful."

As we exited the funeral home, I noticed a police cruiser parked in the back of the empty lot.

"Who do you think that is?" Ruby asked.

"I don't know," I replied. The glare from the sun hitting the windshield didn't allow me to see inside. "They're probably doing the same thing we are—looking at who attended the funeral."

"You're most likely right on that one, Bernie. Too bad they didn't go inside. They'd have a much better view of all the suspects instead of hanging out in the parking lot." Ruby waved and then gave the cops a one finger salute.

"Good thing you're dead or we'd both end up in jail with your antics," I said, sliding into the driver's seat while Ruby laughed.

On our way home, my shoulders sagged as defeat rolled through me. I'd been spinning my wheels trying to obtain information about Stanley's murder, and I still wasn't any closer to discovering the killer. I thought for sure Moonlit Coffin and maybe Ricky had been involved, but I also might have heard Ann confess. Then there was Merry at Joyous Jewels... she had motive as well.

"I like when you wear your mood ring because I don't need to ask you what you're thinking," Ruby said, pointing at my hand. "That black tells me you're all sorts of stressed."

"We should have this figured out by now," I said. "Maybe I should take everything I know and go to Adam. Leave solving the case to the professional."

"Nah. It'll come together for us. It always

does. Just let me think a bit about our next move."

As we rounded the corner to my house, I saw Jack's car parked out front. "I wonder what he wants."

Darla and Jack stood by the front door and waved as I drove by. "I don't feel like seeing them," I muttered.

"How can you not want to see Mr. Dimples?" Ruby bounced around in her seat. "He's a fine specimen of a man. Appreciate God's art, Bernie!"

I rolled my eyes and pulled into the back lot. With his wavy brown hair, green eyes and bright smile, he was definitely one of the best-looking men in Sedona. Ruby would argue with me and say the world, the dimples cinching the status.

With a sigh, I checked my reflection in the rearview mirror, then exited the car and headed for the back door, Ruby following me while humming a Janis Joplin tune. Once inside, I hurried through the kitchen, dining area, and living room and found my friends still on my front walkway.

"What's going on?" I asked as they filed

in. Darla glanced all around while she pulled off her coat, as if she were looking for something.

"Not a lot," she replied. "We thought we'd stop by and say hi."

Jack had yet to speak to me, but he kept his curious gaze fixed on my face. Did I have something stuck to it? I brushed my cheek looking for the offending particle even though I'd just checked my reflection in the car.

"I told him," Darla said. "I hope you won't be mad, but I couldn't help it."

Oh, no. "Told him... what?"

"About Ruby."

Fully understanding Jack's stare, I smiled away my irritation. Like I didn't have enough on my plate at the moment.

I'd asked Darla not to mention my secret to anyone, but apparently that had gone in one ear and out the other.

Jack narrowed his gaze on me. "I'm not sure what to think about this," he said. "There's no such thing as ghosts."

"Don't tell me I'm not real, buddy," Ruby

said, placing herself right in front of him, her hands on her hips.

"Let me guess," I said, getting right to the point of proving her existence. "Right now you smell lavender and marijuana."

A flicker of recognition crossed his face.

"You've always been my favorite. Don't be a jerk and lose that top spot, hot buns." Ruby snorted.

"You may feel a small gust of cool air," I continued, then Ruby grabbed both his cheeks. "Your face is cold right now."

"If you don't think I exist, you're dumber than a horse's—"

"Holy cow," Jack whispered, stepping away. "Is it true?"

I nodded. "Yep. I couldn't see her until I got back from my cousin's wedding where I was hit by lightning. I know how uncomfortable and discombobulated you feel right now."

It was Jack's turn to glance all around the room. "What... what does she look like? Like a cloud or a mist? Or like Casper?"

I glanced at my ghost. Long gray hair in a ponytail and a purple mumu covering her thin frame. "She looks like she did in life. In fact, when she died she was wearing a purple mumu, so that's what she's stuck with in death."

"And no undies!" Ruby yelled as she pulled up the hem of her dress to her thighs. "Want to take a peek?"

"No!" I yelled. "I don't want to see! No one does!"

Ruby cackled as Jack asked, "See what?"

"Nothing," I replied, shaking my head.

"So the stories of this place being haunted are true," he said. "I always thought it was something you started to bring in more customers."

"I didn't start the rumors," I said. "The guests did. The first reviews noted the strange scents and the blasts of cold that came out of nowhere. I just went along with it."

"Because you couldn't see her?"

"Exactly. I had the same experiences as them, but I just brushed them off. The guests wrote reviews saying they loved it."

"Is she dangerous?"

Ruby raised her arms in the air and

moaned while rolling her eyes to the back of her head. "No," I replied, not bothering to go into the fact that I knew another ghost who could move inanimate objects. But he'd been dead longer than Ruby and I speculated the longer a ghost hung around on this plane, the more powerful they became. I only hoped Ruby would find her resting place before she developed this ability.

"What does she do all day?" Jack asked. "Can she hear me?"

"Of course I can hear you," Ruby said, then moved behind him and started singing *Hot Cross Buns*.

"She hears you." *But it's probably a good thing you can't hear her.* "She mainly makes inappropriate remarks about people... especially men."

"Really?" Jack chuckled. "Like what?"

"Like if I were alive, you and I would be doing the horizontal bop!" Ruby said, shaking her hips in a circular motion.

"Oh, nothing that should be repeated," I replied, a deep blush crawling over my cheeks. Time to change the subject. "Do you guys want something to drink?"

"Sure," Darla said, and we filed into the kitchen.

"I'm not going to lie, but I thought Darla needed her medication adjusted when she shared Ruby with me," Jack said as they sat down on the island stools.

"Nope. Ruby's real," I replied. "But I would appreciate it if we could keep this between us." I eyed Darla warily. "I don't want this getting out."

"I promise!" she said. "I won't tell anyone else."

As they each had a soda, I made more coffee. There wasn't enough caffeine to get me through my day, but I hoped it would help.

"Where have you been?" Darla asked. "You're sure dressed up."

Glancing down at my too-tight skirt and smelly turtleneck, I couldn't wait to change. "I went to Stanley's funeral."

"I didn't know you felt that strongly about his death," Darla said, furrowing her brow.

"Just wanted to pay my respects." As I poured cream into my coffee, I didn't meet her gaze. I reached for the sugar but decided not to have any when the skirt felt it may burst as I sat down.

"Have you spoken to Adam lately?" Jack asked.

I shook my head. "No. Haven't seen him."

"Yeah, he told Stanley's death is a murder investigation. He's really busy."

"Did he say anything else about the case?" I asked as nonchalantly as possible.

Jack shrugged. "Not really. Just that they were looking at a lot of suspects."

I suddenly remembered Jack did repair work on motorcycles for Moonlit Coffin and I had wanted to discuss it with him. "How well do you know Gunner and Thunder from Moonlit Coffin?"

He took a sip of soda before answering while gathering his thoughts. "Overall, they're good guys. Especially Gunner."

Interesting. The one who had threatened me was described as a good guy.

"We talk bikes, parts and rides," Jack said.

"They asked if you wanted to be a prospect," Darla interjected.

"Yeah, that's not for me," Jack said, eyeing me. "I don't want any trouble."

Jack's past included a stint in prison for theft. He'd made it clear he wanted to live a life on the right side of the law, and I wasn't sure if that included staying away from MC clubs. But his stare also made me question whether he'd told Darla about his former life.

"Do you think they're trouble?" I asked. "Do you believe they're dangerous and into illegal things?"

"Beats me," he replied. "Like I said, our chatter is about bike stuff. I don't get into club business with them."

"What *is* their business?" I asked, suddenly realizing I had no idea what an MC club did except ride motorcycles and according to Thunder, charity work. And in the case of Moonlit Coffin, maybe they also murdered lawyers for kicks and giggles.

"They have the Ride for Life," Darla said. "They escort a blood bank truck around the area and encourage people to donate. That's the only thing I've ever heard them talk about when they eat at my place... beside bikes."

"I'm familiar with it," I grumbled. "But do they have jobs? Or does the club generate revenue for them all to live on?"

"Thunder mentioned he worked as a plumber once," Jack offered. "But that's all I can think of."

"What about Gunner? Does anyone know what he does?" I asked.

Jack and Darla exchanged glances and shrugged.

"Hey!" Darla said. "What's the deal for Christmas this year?"

Even though I hadn't finished talking about Moonlit Coffin, I did appreciate the subject change because it was my favorite topic: Christmas.

"Par-tay! Par-tay!" Ruby chanted.

"We're having a party here at the house," I said. "Of course, you two are invited."

"Oh, how fun!" Darla squealed. "Are you going to decorate again?"

"Of course," I said. "I love to do it."

While alive, Ruby had also enjoyed the

holidays and decorated lavishly. When I moved in and found all the ornaments, I combined them with my own and continued the tradition. This would be the first year we'd participate together since I couldn't see her for the first three years I lived in the house.

"Who else are you going to invite?" Darla asked.

"I'm not sure. I haven't really considered the guest list except you two. Definitely Jezebel." But probably not her bullyish boyfriend Gunner if they were still together. Hopefully not. "We'll see."

"Can I help with the food?" Darla asked.

"I was hoping you'd say that," I replied. "I'd love it if you did."

"Yeah, thanks," Ruby said. "I'd hate to watch people eat cold hotdogs and cheese slices at my big party."

I glared at her and shook my head. It wouldn't be *that* bad if Darla hadn't volunteered.

"And I can help with your decorations," Jack said. "Getting up on ladders is dangerous."

"Perfect. Thank you."

I smiled at my friends, so grateful they were in my life. An hour later, they returned to their respective businesses and Ruby and I were left with the murder hanging between us. The distraction Jack and Darla had offered had been a nice reprieve.

"You better get out of those clothes," Ruby said. "You probably smell like death on top of old beer and fear."

"I don't know where to go from here," I muttered as I strolled into my bedroom.

"Oh, no worries," she called. "I do!"

CHAPTER 13

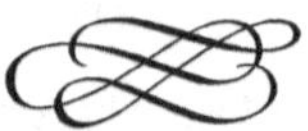

"I DON'T THINK I like this idea," I said as we drove toward the law firm Ricky now owned.

"Why not?" Ruby asked. "You don't have to do anything. Just sit in your car and watch the building. It's called a stakeout."

"We don't know anything about stakeouts."

"How hard can it be? They do it on TV all the time. We just get coffee, park a ways away, and watch for the perp. Just like Cagney and Lacey."

"And what if he leaves the office?"

"Then we follow him. I think you're

making this far harder than it has to be, Bernie."

Maybe it was as simple as grabbing a cup of coffee and sitting in my car, but I still felt exposed and like I was doing something I shouldn't.

"We're skipping the coffee," I grumbled. "I'd have to pee within the hour."

"Okay, but park over there," Ruby said as the law office came into view. "At the back of the lot."

I pulled into a space and Ruby shook her head. "No, silly! You back in! That way if we need to escape, you can do so quickly!"

Valid point.

Ruby sighed and shook her head. "Jeez, Bernie. Are you even paying attention when we're watching Columbo?"

I backed out and re-parked, then shut off the engine and settled in.

"This is a perfect view," she said. "Now we sit back and wait for the weasel to make his appearance."

"We don't even know if he's in there."

"He's in there. I feel it in my dead bones.

He's going to show us exactly who he's involved with."

I glanced around the parking lot trying to predict what car belonged to Ricky. The black Cadillac sedan? Probably not. The beige SUV? Maybe. But my bet was on the red Dodge Charger or the yellow Corvette. He seemed like the type to be attracted to racecars.

Fifteen minutes passed and my eyes started to flutter closed. I really should be at home curled up on my couch instead of sitting in the car with my ghost and her silly plan.

"I have an idea!" Ruby said, startling me so bad I jumped from my seat. "Let's go by the side of the building. I can sneak in a peek and see if he's there."

"You just told me you're certain he is."

"Well, let's be sure because I've discovered stakeouts are boring. They're far more entertaining watching them on the boob tube."

I thoroughly agreed, but to actually walk up to the building and spy in the office windows? It seemed dangerous. "Ruby,

I don't know about that. What if he sees us?"

"What if he does?" she said, shrugging. "You just launch into a tirade about how you need help restructuring your business."

I'd almost forgot about that detail that still needed to be addressed.

"Easy peasy, super squeezy."

"Fine," I muttered. "Let's do it." If I didn't get moving, I'd be asleep in minutes.

As we strode across the parking lot, Ruby spun in circles next to me while I pulled my coat tighter. Winter was definitely on the way but the cool air helped revive my senses.

"Okay, stay here," she said. "Lean against the building like you're waiting for someone. Keep it casual."

I stood right next to the window. Anyone inside the office who peered out wouldn't be able to see me and anyone who spotted me from the parking lot... well, I wouldn't be surprised if I got arrested for loitering or prostitution.

Ruby looked in the window. "He's got a new secretary," she said. "Young thing. How in the heck does she reach the keyboard with those big boobies?"

I didn't answer but instead smiled at the woman passing by.

"Ricky's in there," Ruby continued. "He's talking to the new girl. Gosh, is he actually flexing his bicep while handing her a file folder? That guy is sure full of himself. Do you think he's on steroids?"

"We know he's in there," I whispered. "Maybe we should head back to the car."

"Hang on. He just went down the hallway to his office, which used to be Stanley's. Let's see what he does next."

Seconds passed then Ruby yelled, "Abort! Abort! He's got his coat and he's heading our way!"

I hurried down the sidewalk to the next business which happened to be a clothing store. Darting out into the parking lot would certainly bring unwanted attention to me.

"Window shop! Window shop!" Ruby screeched.

Great idea.

As I shoved my hands into my coat

pocket, I turned to the window and studied the display of frilly dresses and heels. Nothing I would wear, but I found them pretty. I tried to imagine myself in the pink ruffles and almost laughed out loud.

"Look! We can spy on him in the window reflection."

I glanced up. Ricky confidently strode across the parking lot toward where the Corvette and Charger were parked. Which one was his?

As he slipped into the red Charger and fired up the engine, Ruby groaned. "That thing's loud. We shouldn't have any trouble tailing him, even if we lose the visual."

I nodded in agreement, then we hurried back to my SUV and followed him out of the parking lot.

"Make sure to stay two cars behind him," Ruby said. "That's what they do on television."

I doubted Ricky was paying attention to anything but his own egocentric thoughts and his reflection in the rearview mirror, but I did as instructed.

"Oh, this is exciting," Ruby said, rubbing

her hands together. "Look out, Cagney and Lacey! Ruby and Bernie are on the case!"

What following Ricky would show us, I had no idea. However, I also realized sulking around my house wouldn't bring us any closer to solving Stanley's murder. When Ruby had come up with the idea of a stakeout, I'd readily agreed. I had nothing better to do… except laundry.

I pulled over to the side of the road when Ricky entered the parking lot of a small warehouse. The sign out front read Pipes and Plumbing. Hadn't Jack mentioned Thunder being a plumber?

And on cue, Thunder walked out of the building wearing his MC cut and a white long-sleeved shirt over his jeans and military boots. They shook hands and then strode back into the building again. A few moments later, three motorcycles pulled in and parked. I didn't recognize any of the riders.

"Do you think this is the Moonlit Coffin clubhouse or something?" Ruby asked.

In my rearview mirror, I noted two other motorcycles rumbling down the street and I slouched down so my head was level with the bottom of the window. "It sure seems that way."

For twenty minutes, we watched bikers come and go until Ricky emerged carrying a black duffel bag. He threw it in his car and sped off.

"We're in hot pursuit!" Ruby yelled as I counted to ten before pulling away from the side of the street.

I didn't bother correcting her—twenty-five miles per hour wasn't exactly hot pursuit, but she seemed to be enjoying the thought. Nervous butterflies tickled my belly as Ricky headed toward the downtown area again. With the traffic getting thicker, I gripped the steering wheel, afraid I'd lose him.

"What's the worm up to?" Ruby mused. "What do you think is in the bag?"

"Beats me."

"Maybe it's money? Like a payoff for something?"

"For what? Legal services? Why not just write a check?"

Ruby shrugged. "Maybe Moonlit Coffin

doesn't have a checking account. Not everyone can be a preferred member of the Bank of Sedona."

"I wish we knew what was in the bag," I muttered. All sorts of things went through my mind: guns, money, drugs, body parts…

When Ricky entered a parking lot behind one of the buildings, I did as well. I maneuvered my SUV as far away from him as possible and watched him in my rearview mirror. As he exited the Charger, Ruby yelled, "Let's go!"

I pushed open the door, hurried over to his car, and tried to yank the door open. Locked.

"What in the world's gotten into you?" Ruby shouted. "That's breaking and entering! You can't break the law! If they haul you to jail, I'm *not* going with you and that means I can't leave the house! Have some courtesy for your dead grandma for goodness' sake!"

Apparently, *my* best interests came in last place even though I was the one with a beating heart.

I ran across the parking lot to the side of

the building, which led to the shops. After peeking around the corner to make sure Ricky wasn't waiting for me, I stepped out into the foot traffic and headed to my left.

"Where'd he go?" Ruby asked. "I don't see him!"

"Me neither," I whispered.

"Wait a minute," she said, coming to a standstill. "Isn't that Joyous Jewels up there?"

She was right.

"What are the chances that Ricky's shining Merry's pretty things?" Ruby mused. "If I'm right, that's the scandal of the week!"

I shook my head. No way. It added too many kinks in the theories I had developed and turned the investigation upside down. "He had to go somewhere else."

"Like where? He doesn't seem to be the type to visit the candy store or the essential oil lady."

A few people turned their heads and gave me strange looks, but I was beyond caring. If they thought I was the mentally unstable woman who stood in the middle of a crowd talking to herself, then so be it. Ruby and I weaved in and out of the throngs and I glanced in every store we passed, hoping to catch a glimpse of the lawyer. No sign of him.

I slowed when we arrived at Joyous Jewels.

"Don't let them see you spying," Ruby said. "I'm betting he's in there."

As I stared in the window, I only saw displays of jewelry. I continued my leisurely stroll, my gaze fixed on the inside of the store while trying to see past the reflections on the glass.

I gasped when my gaze locked onto the back of the building. There stood Ricky and Merry embracing, their mouths moving in a passionate kiss, almost completely hidden by the displays and the partially closed curtain that separated the front of the store from the back.

"Well, he's curling her toes," Ruby commented. "Wasn't she all upset today at the funeral?"

She had been. Tears of grief she hadn't tried to hide streamed down her face. I couldn't tear my gaze away from them as the sheer audacity of the two seeped in. Even though Stanley was dead and most likely in the ground, I stood stunned at the utter betrayal from two of the closest people in his life—his girlfriend and his partner.

Remaining completely fixated, I didn't hear anyone come up behind me.

"I've been looking for you," a voice growled from behind me as a thick hand grasped my bicep. "We need to talk."

My first instinct was to fight and I tried to get away, but he held tight.

"Police brutality!" Ruby shouted. "Police brutality! Get off her, copper!"

I turned to find myself face-to-face with Adam, and the adrenaline slowly ebbed. We may not be a couple any longer, but I knew in my soul he wouldn't hurt me.

His furious glare shrunk my bravery for a moment, but then I straightened my spine and pulled my arm away. "What's wrong with you?" I hissed. "Don't sneak up on me like that."

"I didn't. You and I need to go some-where private to talk."

Turning away from him, I hurried back toward my car. "You can call me later."

"Yeah," Ruby yelled, trailing behind me. "Call and make an appointment. Maybe next month she'll have some time for you!"

"No, Bernie," he said, catching up to me in a few long strides. "This can't wait. Your life's in danger and you need to know the truth before you get hurt."

CHAPTER 14

WE RETURNED TO MY HOUSE. My hands shook as I made a pot of coffee. His presence gave me a thrill, as well as the curling in my stomach of utter dread. Of course, I was still slightly irritated he hadn't stuck up for me when the sheriff asked him if I'd been the one to kill Stanley.

Once we both had our cups of ambition, we filed into the living room. Adam sank into the couch across from me, his shoulders sagging, and pursed his lips. He set down his mug and sighed. Defeat.

"He doesn't look happy," Ruby said, and I had to agree.

"I was going to have you arrested for interfering with an investigation to protect you, but I couldn't," he said. "I still care about you, Bernie, and I'm very afraid of what's going to happen to you."

Yay! He cared about me. But, boo... what had I gotten myself into if he wanted to *arrest* me in order to *protect* me?

"What have I done?" I asked. "I haven't broken any laws."

"No, you haven't," he replied. "Which is a good thing."

I blew on the hot liquid and took a sip. "So, what's going on?"

"First, I need you to tell me why you're trying to solve Stanley's murder."

"I'm not."

Adam rolled his eyes. "Don't lie to me, Bernie. Please. It's insulting."

"Well, the cat's out of the bag on this one," Ruby said. "May as well be honest."

"It was Ruby's idea," I said softly, unable to meet his gaze. "At first, I wasn't trying to solve it—I promise. I wanted nothing to do with it. But then Ruby and I saw some things we shouldn't have and... we decided that if I could give you information on the case that you didn't have, then maybe… maybe you'd realize how amazing I am and you'd want me back."

Saying everything out loud made the plan sound so incredibly silly. A deep blush crawled over my cheeks and down my neck. An earthquake or the floor swallowing me up would've been appreciated.

"But it turned into something more," I continued. "I wanted to bring you the murderer's name and all the evidence. I wanted to find Stanley's killer to prove that I could. I wanted to best the sheriff's office."

Jeez. How pathetic. Level Ten Pettiness.

Adam sighed and sat back against the cushions, staring up at the ceiling. Long moments passed while I studied his chin. He hadn't shaved in a couple of days and the blond stubble looked good on him. If we hadn't been in the middle of the most uncomfortable conversation of my life, I may have mentioned it.

"You're so far in the deep end you're practically drowning, Bernie," Adam finally said. "The only way out of this that I can see is honesty."

Huh. I obviously hadn't realized I was in any trouble. The truth was always nice, but it added to the discomfort raging through me. "Okay..."

"Gunner isn't a killer," Adam said, sighing again. "In fact, he's an undercover cop."

Speechless, I simply stared. Gunner? An undercover cop? The big Black dude with tattoos, bald head, and thick beard?

"He's been in place within Moonlit Coffin for about five years now. It's taken a long time for him to climb to the level he's at within the organization and you poking your nose where it doesn't belong is not only putting him in danger, but you as well."

"I really didn't see that one coming," Ruby said. "Wow. That's nuts. If I wasn't dead, I'd have to sit down."

"Uh... I'm not sure what to say," I whispered. "I had no idea. How... how did you know I talked to Gunner?"

"He called me when he found out you and I used to date," Adam replied. "He hoped I could talk some sense into you."

I'd basically accused an undercover cop

of murder. How... unprofessional and juvenile. "He must think I'm the biggest idiot alive."

"No, he doesn't. He found you quite amusing, but at the same time, he knew you could be putting yourself in danger, as well as him. When he saw you at Stanley's funeral, he realized you weren't going to step aside, despite his threats. He called me."

"How did he find out you and I used to date?"

"Jezebel."

"Does she know?" I asked. "About Gunner?"

Adam nodded. "That's why she tried to steer you away from him."

"Why didn't she say something?" I asked, feeling even more ridiculous. "Why didn't she just tell me the truth?!"

"She can't, Bernie," Adam replied. "It's top-secret information, and you'll have to make sure not to repeat it."

I nodded and rubbed my temples with my forefingers, embarrassment still raging through me. "Are they even a real couple?"

"Yes. Gunner says his involvement with

Moonlit Coffin worries Jezebel, and sometimes the stress gets to be too much and they break up. But they always end up getting back together. It helps that the MC members like to hang out at her bar. She keeps an eye on him."

I shook my head as tears welled in my eyes. I had been the odd one out on a huge secret even though I had no right to know. "I feel so stupid."

"Don't," Adam said. In three strides he was at my side, his arm around my shoulders. "There's a reason why you weren't aware of any of it: you aren't in law enforcement. The rule when it comes to undercover operations is the fewer people involved, the better. *I* don't even know the full story about his investigation into the MC. He reports directly to the Sheriff. I'm just aware of bits and pieces."

"What's Moonlit Coffin done?" I asked. "Why are they being investigated?"

"They've been on the radar for a number of years. We believe they're part of a big drug ring that spans four states, but we don't have the proof. They're an incredibly tight-knit group. Gunner's been trying to gather the evidence but gaining the trust of the club has taken years. And now, we're looking at them for Stanley's murder."

I nodded. "I'm so dumb," I repeated.

"You're not," Adam said. "You're a very bright, intelligent woman who was out of her league. We had to level with you so you wouldn't get yourself hurt or Gunner killed. If they find out he's police, they'll probably take him out to the desert and shoot him."

I'd never recover if I were responsible for someone's murder, especially a police officer's. And all because I was playing Nancy Drew, something I had no business doing.

Leaning my head against Adam's shoulder, I relished in the contact, the security and safety it brought. I was home. "I'm sorry, Adam," I said. "I'm sorry for... for everything. For getting involved in Stanley's case, for breaking into your house... I'm like a wrecking ball swinging around and trying to destroy everything in my way."

"Don't be so hard on yourself," he said.

"You couldn't have known about Gunner. If you did, we'd have a bigger problem."

"What's that?"

"A leak in the police department and probably a dead officer."

"Oh, my gosh! How awful!"

"You didn't seem surprised when I said Stanley had been killed," Adam murmured. "How did you know?"

"You and the sheriff were talking about it the day I found the body," I replied. "Then Penny confirmed it when I had coffee with her. She said she'd spoken with your department about it."

"Penny does like to talk. Longest interview I've ever witnessed. Did you know it's illegal to own one guinea pig in Switzerland?"

"What?" I asked, laughing.

"Yes. Penny told me and I actually looked it up to verify after the interview."

"Why is that?"

"They're very social animals and they consider it cruelty to only own one."

I appreciated the kindness of the law and remembered Penny's tangent on blue-eyed people when we'd had coffee. "How did the discussion veer onto guinea pigs?"

"I'm still wondering the same thing," he said, kissing the top of my head. "This feels nice. I've missed you."

I nodded and snuggled in closer.

"Are you... seeing anyone?" he asked.

When Adam had broken up with me, I'd pretty much given up on men. My track record before him had been mediocre at best. "No."

After a long stretch of silence, he said, "Do you... do you think we should try to be together again?"

I startled into an upright position and banged my head into his chin. "I'm so sorry!" I said as he moaned and blood pooled on his lips. "Oh, my word. Let me fetch a paper towel."

Leave it to me to ruin what could have been one the most romantic moments of my life. A tender kiss. A warm embrace. Promises of the future. Instead, I hurried into the kitchen. Adam wanted to get back together! "I can't believe this," I whispered as I wetted the paper towel.

"You better play it cool," Ruby said, appearing next to me. "Don't be too eager. Make him work for it."

"But I was the one who screwed up the relationship in the first place!" I hissed. *Because of you! I should be begging him to take me back!*"

"So now it's my fault you broke into his condo?"

I glared at my ghost, wanting to throttle her. She may have a point, but I didn't have the will or the time to argue with her. "It *was* your idea."

"Yeah, but you didn't have to go along with my silly plan," she replied, laughing. "Take some responsibility for your actions, Bernie. I just planted the seed. You brought the plan to fruition. I'll leave you two to work things out."

She vanished and I stared at where she'd been standing, once again wondering if she was a figment of my imagination. The yin to my yang. My Jekyll to my Mr. Hyde. The little devil sitting on my shoulder, encouraging me to do things I shouldn't. However, there wasn't time for any deep introspection. I had a bloody cop I desperately wanted to kiss waiting in my living room.

"I'm so sorry about this, Adam," I blurted when I returned to his side. His lips swelled as I dabbed at the blood. "I guess I got excited."

"Does that mean yes?" he asked, taking the paper towel from me. "Do you want to try again?"

I nodded and sank down into the cushion next to him. "Breaking into your condo was wrong," I said. "I'm very aware of that and I've beat myself up for it more than you could ever know. But I was so worried about Darla. I was afraid she'd commit suicide or be admitted into the hospital. She was in a bad place and the stress of the investigation was too much for her. I had to help her."

His blue eyes twinkled as he smiled. "I appreciate your loyalty to your friend."

"I'd do the same for you. I'd walk across glass if you asked me to."

"Well, I never would," Adam said, chuckling. He pulled away the paper towel to reveal a very swollen lip.

"That doesn't look good."

"Is it a deal breaker?"

"No." I shook my head. "Not at all."

Adam leaned in and gave me a soft kiss. "That hurts," he whispered, cringing. "We'll have to try again later."

"I can't wait," I replied. With a grin, I curled up against him again and placed my head on his shoulder as my heart grew wings and happy tears once again pricked my eyes. Adam had decided to give me another chance, and this time, I wouldn't screw it up by listening to Ruby and her crazy ideas. He and I were so good together, I wouldn't ruin my relationship with him again.

Adam cleared his throat. "In the meantime, why don't you tell me what you've discovered while poking your nose in places it doesn't belong?"

"It may be best if we share information," I said. "Not to be difficult, but I believe two heads are better than one when it comes to solving a murder."

He sighed. After a long moment, he said, "Let me grab my laptop from the car."

CHAPTER 15

ADAM OPENED THE DEVICE, waited for it to fire up, then typed in his passcode. A few more keystrokes and he was in the sheriff's department website pulling up statements.

"Here's Penny's," he said. "You can skip over the parts where she veers off topic. Those are marked with a red asterisk."

"She seems to do that a lot," I muttered as I took the laptop and leaned against the cushions.

PENNY: *The morning of Stanley's death, I arrived at the office around seven thirty and started a pot of coffee. I gathered the client files*

Stanley would need for the day and set them on his desk. He came in at his usual time—around eight—and we reviewed his schedule. His first client arrived about twenty minutes after.

Ricky, being the lazy-daisy he is, didn't arrive until almost nine-thirty. I don't know what time zone he's living in, but it's disrespectful to the office.

Deputy: *Is there a certain time he's supposed to be in?*

Penny: *Not that I'm aware, but the early bird gets the worm. You should know that, Deputy.*

Deputy: *Did you pull files for Ricky as well?*
Penny: *No.*
Deputy: *Why is that?*
Penny: *He takes care of his own files.*

"She didn't like Ricky," I said, meeting his blue gaze as he dabbed his lip again. "She made that really clear to me."

Adam nodded. "Yeah, that was very obvious. Reading the interview doesn't quite catch the disdain she has toward him. She sneered almost every time his name came up."

PENNY: *The morning went by smoothly with quite a few phone calls and clients coming in.*
    Deputy: *Clients for both Stanley and Ricky?*
    Penny: *Mainly Stanley, but a few for Ricky. He's so unlikeable, I can't imagine anyone wanting him to do any work for them. For such a small office, it was surprisingly busy. We were booked all morning and into the afternoon. And Ricky had the audacity to complain about it, saying he was made for more than wills and forming LLCs.*

GLANCING UP AT ADAM, I said, "I had an appointment that day."

"Yes. You told me that when I arrived at the scene and I also saw your name on the calendar."

"While I was sitting with Ricky in the reception area, he told me he hated that Penny used a paper calendar. Said it was right out of the Stone Age and called her and Stanley tree killers."

"He didn't like much about that office, did he?"

I shook my head and returned to reading.

PENNY: *Around noon, I made more coffee. I'd mentioned to Stanley many times that he'd sleep better and have less indigestion if he didn't have coffee during the afternoon, but he continued to drink it. Good thing I kept a stash of antacid. Every day around four without fail he complained about heartburn.*

Deputy: *I have your calendar here. Can we go over the names of these people who came in before lunch?*

Penny: *Sure.*

"YOU CAN SKIP over most of that," Adam said. "We're checking them, but most have been ruled out. I feel it was someone who came in after lunch. Someone close to him."

"Who?"

He chuckled and lightly gripped the tip of my nose between his knuckles. "Keep reading, and you tell me."

PENNY: *Merry from Joyous Jewels stopped by just as I was making the afternoon pot of coffee. I guess I can say this now that he's dead, but I think he was having an affair with her.*

Deputy: *Really? Are you a hundred percent certain?*

Penny: *No. Maybe ninety-five. I've been with Stanley for thirty years and he's always had some secret young thing.*

Deputy: *What about his wife?*

Penny: *Ann. A lovely woman who doesn't deserve to be treated so callously.*

Deputy: *Did she know about his affairs?*

Penny: *I believe so. How could she not? She never caused a scene, though. She was always kind to me. For my first Christmas at the office, she brought me a charm bracelet. Every year after, she gave me another charm. I sounded like Santa's sleigh walking around the office!*

Deputy: *That was nice of her.*

Penny: *Yes. Sometimes she'd show up at*

closing and bring a bottle of wine for me and her to share. I believe she was lonely because although she was married, Stanley was always emotionally attached elsewhere.

Deputy: Tell me about Merry from Joyous Jewels. You said she came by that day.

Penny: Yes. She came in but didn't stay long. When she left, she seemed upset.

Deputy: Do you know what about?

Penny: No. Stanley took her back to the office and they chatted for a few moments behind a closed door. I didn't hear any of the conversation. I recall being so happy she left when she did because Ann showed up minutes after she walked out the door.

Deputy: That must have been uncomfortable.

Penny: I'm used to it.

Deputy: Can you tell me what happened?

Penny: I had just made Stanley's cup of coffee and one for Ricky as well. I don't like the man, but I do try to remain polite. Ann took a mug back to Stanley's office after we chatted a moment. They also had a private conversation—that was until Ricky barged in when Ann was using the restroom.

Deputy: *Do you know what Stanley and Ricky discussed while Ann was away from the office?*

Penny: *Yes. There was no civilized, closed-door conversation between the two of them. Ricky was discussing taking the biker gang, Moonlit Coffin, on as a client. Stanley wanted no part of it. He loudly made that known.*

Deputy: *Sounds like a rough day at the office for you, Penny.*

Penny: *It wasn't that bad until those scary men from Moonlit Coffin walked in. Thankfully, I left shortly after.*

"WE PASSED her when she returned to the office," I said. "She looked absolutely shocked to see the police there."

"I thought the poor woman was going to drop dead of a heart attack when I explained what had happened that day," Adam said. "First she was hysterically crying, but then she yelled at Ricky and told him it was all his fault."

"Why would she do that?" I asked. "Do you think she knows something?"

"Sure she does," Ruby said. "She's aware Ricky's a slimeball."

I turned to my ghost. "I thought you were going to leave us alone."

"Well, I thought you'd be doing all sorts of kissy stuff, not talking about murder."

"Hi, Ruby," Adam said.

"Hey, copper. It's good to see you back in my granddaughter's arms. You belong there. Don't screw it up again."

"She says hello," I said, not bothering to correct her again that I was the one who'd created the mess in the relationship before.

"So, what do you think?" Adam asked, pointing to the computer.

"Well, when I was there, I overheard you and the sheriff talking and he believed Stanley was poisoned with Penny's eyedrops."

"That's true."

"How did it happen?"

"It was in the coffee cup," Adam replied. "The one sitting on his desk when he died."

I recalled seeing the coffee pot on. "So it wasn't in the pot. Just his cup?"

"Yes."

"It was meant for him then."

"Exactly."

I set down the computer and leaned back against the cushions. "And basically, everyone who could want Stanley dead had access to him and his cup on the day he died."

"Agreed."

"So, who do you think killed him?"

I turned to Adam as he ran a hand through his blond hair. "His wife could've wanted him dead. Merry might have as well because apparently they weren't together any longer."

"But Stanley was writing her an email stating he wanted to get back together with her."

"You noticed that when you found the body?"

"Yes," I lied. Ruby was the one who had seen the computer screen, not me. But she'd also insisted that I tell Adam she wasn't at the lawyer's office that day. "I did see it." A wave of guilt washed through me but I pushed it away and let it pass. Going forward, truth would be my middle name where Adam was concerned. "However, today I also witnessed Merry and Ricky locked in a pretty intense kiss at her store."

Adam's eyes widened. "Really?"

"Yes. And if you think about it, they've got a perfect motive. First, Ricky gets the office and can do with it as he pleases since he's a partner. Second, Merry is rid of Stanley and she probably owns the store outright. And third, they no longer have to hide their affair."

"But Merry… I don't know. Her interview was anything but contentious. In fact, I'd say she's soft-spoken and incapable of killing anything, let alone a former lover."

"She wanted him dead though," Ruby said. "Make sure you tell him that."

I nodded. "Ruby saw Merry's diary when we were in the store. She said she wanted Stanley dead."

"That was in the diary?"

"Yes."

Adam sighed and rubbed the stubble on his chin. "Oh, man. I never… I never expected that. I can't use it as evidence, though, since I can't say a ghost came across the diary."

"I know, but Stanley was part owner in the store and she was having an affair with him. As Ruby pointed out, Stanley wasn't exactly a silver fox. Why would a young, pretty woman sleep with a guy like that unless she had to?"

"You mean money for the store?"

"Right. It's a win-win for both."

Adam exhaled a breath and stood. As he paced the length of the couch, I watched silently.

"You can practically see the squirrel spinning on that wheel in there," Ruby said, marching next to him, her legs passing through the coffee table.

"It's a hamster," I muttered.

"How does a hamster fit into this case?" Adam asked.

"It doesn't," I replied. "Ruby said… never mind. It's not important."

Adam chuckled and shook his head. "She's walking right next to me, isn't she?"

"Yes."

He stuck out his tongue in her general

direction, which sent her into fits of giggles. Ruby loved it when he acknowledged her existence.

"What about Moonlit Coffin?" I asked. "What did they have to say when you interviewed them?"

"Thunder had nothing to say. Denied he'd been there, despite that Penny verified he'd been present. Gunner also confirmed they'd been there. According to him, Thunder really got into Stanley's face when he said his firm wouldn't represent a bunch of hooligans."

Being on the receiving end of Thunder's tirades made me cringe. Both he and Gunner had scared me. "Thunder could've easily squeezed eyedrops into Stanley's cup."

"Yeah, and according to Gunner, Thunder has a dry-eye condition that requires him to carry them."

Stunned, I stared at Adam for a brief second. "Why haven't you arrested him? Stanley died from eyedrop poisoning and Thunder carries them in his pocket?"

"He's our best bet," he replied, continuing his pacing. "But we're trying to put the pieces together to make sure we catch everyone involved. And besides that, if we arrest Thunder, we don't know what will happen to Gunner. He's got Thunder's trust right now, but all that could change if the man gets put away. It could mean a five-year investigation down the drain. Do we pick up a *potential* murderer and possibly lose our chance to bust a drug ring spanning four states?"

I understood his point, but at the same time, it seemed they had Thunder for the killing hook, line, and sinker.

"So, the murder weapon probably *wasn't* Penny's eyedrops," I muttered.

"Nope. But murdering a lawyer because he didn't want his office to represent you?" Adam shook his head. "It seems so excessive."

"And it doesn't seem very gang-ish," I pointed out. "I would expect death by tire iron or gunshot from the leader of a motor-cycle club."

"Maybe he's really smart and takes care of his business in the way that draws the least attention. There has to be more to it."

Adam plopped down on the cushion next to me. "I think Ricky's behind it. He had Thunder do it."

"But what does Gunner say? Does he think Moonlit Coffin killed Stanley?" I asked. "Wouldn't he know since he's number two in the club?"

"He has no knowledge of it, but that doesn't mean it didn't happen," Adam replied. "According to Gunner, Thunder could've sanctioned it without him knowing. If that's the case, I want to get everyone responsible."

"Which means Ricky, if your theory is right."

"Yes. I want to be able to catch him in the sweep of arrests when it goes down, so I want to nail down his motive."

"Well, he's got two. With Stanley out of the way, he gets the office and he gets Merry."

CHAPTER 16

"Mᴀʏ I ʀᴇᴀᴅ Aɴɴ's sᴛᴀᴛᴇᴍᴇɴᴛ?" I asked.

"Sure," Adam replied as he took the laptop from me. "She's another good candidate."

"Let me guess: wife at the end of her rope after dealing with a cheating husband for so many years?"

"Exactly. And as you mentioned, murder by poison is more of a woman's way of killing instead of a biker gang's modus operandi."

"Even though I said that, it sounds a little sexist coming from you."

Adam shrugged and handed me the laptop. "Whether it's sexist or not, it's fact.

Throughout history it's been proven again and again women kill more stealthily than men."

I nodded, then recalled something Penny had said. "When Penny and I had coffee, she mentioned Ann had worn a turquoise necklace once."

"And?" He looked so cute when he furrowed his brow.

"And Joyous Jewels carries a lot of turquoise pieces. I bet Stanley brought it home for her one day after a visit with Merry."

He stared at me a long moment and shook his head. "I'm not following what that has to do with the murder."

"Nothing really," I replied, shrugging. "It reaffirms Stanley was a big jerk. Bringing home a piece of jewelry to your wife from your girlfriend's store? That's pretty low."

"Ah, I see," Adam replied. "You're right."

"Low as you can go," Ruby chimed in. "But old Stanley was still a good guy in my book."

"And, it only adds more fuel to the theory that Ann killed him," I said. "It gives her more reason to. I wonder why she stayed with him."

"Maybe it was easier for her," Ruby said. "Divorces can get messy, especially when one of them is a lawyer."

"Did they have kids?" I asked.

Ruby shook her head. "Not that I know of. No one ever mentioned them and I don't recall ever seeing any pictures in the office."

"Ann said they never did," Adam confirmed.

It was odd having the same conversation with two people who couldn't hear each other, but I'd had a lot of practice before the breakup. In fact, I realized it was another part of Adam missing from my life that had seemed off this past month with just Ruby and me.

"Why remain in a marriage spanning decades with an unfaithful husband?" I asked. Neither my ghost nor my boyfriend (eek!) had an answer for me.

"Read the statement," Adam said, pointing to the computer in my lap. "Then let's talk about it."

· · ·

DEPUTY: *I'm sorry for your loss, Mrs. Jones.*
Ann: *Thank you.*
Deputy: *What can you tell me about the day of Stanley's death?*
Ann: *Well, I went to visit Stanley shortly after lunch to check in. Penny told me he'd had a very busy morning and she was about to bring him and Rick some afternoon coffee. I took one for Stanley and brought it to him.*

"IF ANN HAD THE CUP, she could've spiked it before giving it to him," I said, bouncing excitedly in my chair. "Poisoning him would've been so easy to do because Stanley's office is at the end of the hall. No one would've seen her pull eyedrops from her pocket and dump them in!"

Adam chuckled and dabbed his lip again. "That's very true. Keep reading, though."

DEPUTY: *You mean Ricky?*
Ann: *Rick, Ricky, whatever. To me a grown man should be called by a grown name. Ricky sounds so childish, especially for a lawyer.*

Deputy: *What do you think of him? Were you happy when your husband brought him on?*

Ann: *Stanley was working too many hours a week for a man his age, so yes, I was happy he wanted to hire someone. I thought bringing Rick on board would mean we would finally do the traveling he'd been promising me, but it didn't. It only meant more stress for him.*

"SEE?" I said. "And now she can travel!"

"She could've traveled beforehand," Adam said. "Just because they were married didn't mean she couldn't do her own thing."

"Right, but if he made promises to her and broke them and was cheating for so many years... it could've been the final nail in his coffin, so to speak."

"Maybe... but I still like Ricky and Thunder for the job. Ricky has a solid motive and gets more out of Stanley's death."

Not sure about any of it, I returned my attention to the statement.

· · ·

DEPUTY: *When he brought on Ricky, what made it more stressful?*

Ann: *He was supposed to help with the workload. Stanley was a fixture in this town for over thirty years and had a long list of clients who not only used him regularly, but also recommended him to others.*

At seventy-five, he'd had enough and finally admitted he needed assistance. Despite his annoying swagger, Rick had the qualifications and was thrilled at first to be at the firm. But once he was made partner, he did nothing but complain about the work. He wanted to take the office in another direction and do criminal law work, something Stanley vehemently declined. He didn't want to mess with the criminal element. And, this is Sedona. It's not like we have a bunch of lawless hooligans running around, except for that biker gang.

Deputy: *Why do you think Ricky suddenly wanted to represent criminals?*

Ann: *I have no idea, except for maybe money. Criminal lawyers usually make more money. Stanley was perfectly content with the mundane.*

Deputy: *This is a difficult subject to broach,*

but the evidence says your husband was having an affair.

Ann: *Yes. Merry is her name, I believe. He's had many over the course of our marriage.*

Deputy: *This may seem like a harsh question but why did you stay?*

Ann: *I couldn't be everything Stanley needed, but we did have a bond. We needed each other.*

Deputy: *In what way?*

Ann: *Are you married?*

Deputy: *No.*

Ann: *Then it would be hard to understand. There are many facets to marriage: a deep friendship, if the two people involved are lucky. There's intelligence compatibility, as well as humor and political compatibility. And of course, physical attraction. Stanley and I shared everything except the physical attraction. Other than that, we were perfectly matched.*

Deputy: *Did his affairs bother you?*

Ann: *Of course. I considered leaving many times. However, it would have been akin to cutting off my right arm. Over time, I decided to ignore his dalliances and enjoy the relationship we did share.*

Deputy: *Ann, are you sad your husband is gone?*

Ann: *I won't lie, Deputy. There is a small part of me that is relieved. I've held my head high as people whispered behind my back. I'm no longer the subject of gossip for our friends, and this will be the last time I have to explain my marriage to anyone.*

Deputy: *What about money?*

Ann: *What do you mean?*

Deputy: *I'm waiting for your bank records, but I'm assuming you two have saved quite a bit?*

Ann: *We've lived well within our means. We hardly ever ate out, except for special occasions. We didn't buy lavish gifts for each other. In fact, we loved to exchange books and discuss them. As I mentioned before, we didn't travel and we had no children. If you're asking if I have any financial concerns, the answer is no.*

I GLANCED AT ADAM. "Did you get their bank records?"

"Yes. Ann is now a multi-millionaire."

"Who wants to travel but never did because of her husband."

"Ann can do whatever she wants," Adam replied. "She can go live in Paris, scour the jungles of the Amazon, or explore Antarctica."

"Why in the world would she want to go to the Antarctic?" I asked, furrowing my brow. "It's so cold!"

"For some people, that would be the adventure of a lifetime," Adam replied. "I'm not saying it's the case with Ann or anyone else who lives in Arizona, most of whom hate being cold. I'm making the point that Ann has no limitations on what she can and can't do based on her bank account."

"Lucky lady," Ruby said dreamily. "It's one heck of a motive to get rid of the old coot. That and her pride. It's got to be hard turning your back on a cheating mongrel all those years."

"You just said he was a good guy," I replied. "So, what is it? A good guy or a cheating mongrel?"

Ruby shrugged. "Everyone has their faults and apparently Stanley's was keeping his pants zipped. But that didn't make him *all* bad."

"Did she just call Stanley a mongrel?" Adam asked, chuckling.

"Yes. In the same sentence she said he wasn't all bad."

Adam shook his head. "I've missed you. Both of you."

"Aww... the copper's trying to get on my good side," Ruby said, batting her eyelashes at him. "He's not quite there, though."

I smiled at him. "I've missed you as well," I whispered as my heart swelled with joy. "And I'm so sorry—"

Adam grabbed my hand. "Let's not talk about that anymore, okay?"

If he wanted to move forward instead of dwelling on the past, I could as well. I nodded and returned to my reading.

DEPUTY: *Are you retired?*

Ann: *Stanley never wanted me to work. I've taken care of our home since the day we were married.*

Deputy: *What about the law office?*

Ann: What about it?

Deputy: Did you ever work there?

Ann: At the beginning of our marriage, I sometimes helped with filing, but when Penny was hired, she took over.

Deputy: What happens to the business now Stanley's gone?

Ann: Rick is a partner. The way the arrangement is set up, I have no claim to any proceeds the office may bring in after his death. I do, however, own the building.

Deputy: Why was the agreement with Ricky structured like that?

Ann: From what I understand, it's a common practice. Besides, I have no way to serve Stanley's clients since I'm not a lawyer. We also had hoped Rick would eventually buy out Stanley.

Deputy: Was the subject ever broached with Ricky?

Ann: I have no idea. Stanley never mentioned it to me if it was.

Deputy: What do you plan on doing with the building?

Ann: I don't know yet. I'd like to bury my husband before making any decisions.

. . .

OBVIOUSLY, the interview had been conducted before the funeral and I wondered if she'd come to any decisions on the property since I'd overheard her in the funeral restroom.

"See, I think maybe Stanley did discuss the buyout with Ricky and it's another reason for Ricky to kill him," I said, liking the man for the murder more and more. "He didn't have to shell out any cash, but he still got the office."

DEPUTY: *Getting back to the day of the murder, how long did you stay and talk with Stanley?*

Ann: *Maybe twenty minutes.*

Deputy: *What did you two discuss?*

Ann: *Well, let's see. The lawn needed to be reseeded and I also had the roof inspected that morning and they found a small leak. We talked about getting a second estimate on fixing it and if Stanley wanted to take on the lawn himself or hire someone to do it for us.*

Deputy: *Why didn't you call?*

Ann: Because I wanted to get out of the house and see Stanley. As I stated before, deputy, our relationship was complicated during the best of times. To an outsider it must have looked odd, very non-traditional. But it worked for us.

Deputy: Can you tell me who was there when you left the office that day?

Ann: Yes, of course. Penny was at her desk getting ready to leave on an errand, and Rick was in the reception area greeting two bikers.

Deputy: Did Penny ever mention how she felt about Ricky's association with them?

Ann: Oh, yes. She wasn't happy about it. Not in the least bit. She told Stanley many times it was a bad idea to even allow them into the office.

Deputy: And Stanley agreed.
Ann: Most definitely.
Deputy: Tell me about Penny.

Ann: What about her? She's been there since Stanley opened the office. She's extremely loyal to him and has kept his professional life running for three decades.

Deputy: Would she have any reason for wanting Stanley dead?

Ann: Oh, heavens, no. She didn't appreciate

Rick joining the office, but that's no reason to kill Stanley. It's absurd to even consider it.

I SET down the computer and met Adam's gaze. "Ann does seem like a really good suspect. Ruby had described her as a doormat, but I disagree. I think she's a very strong woman who made the best she could out of a bad situation."

"I'm with you. She's definitely not a doormat. Their marriage was hard to understand, but she got some joy out of it. At least, I hope she did. But maybe she'd just reached her breaking point."

Which reminded me, I had more information Adam didn't. I kind of liked this knowledge swap we had going on. "When I went to the funeral, I was using the restroom and Ann and her sister came in. They were unaware I was there. Ann wasn't upset about Stanley's death in the least bit. In fact, she said she was glad her husband was gone, which led me to believe she most certainly had something to do with the murder."

CHAPTER 17

ADAM SIGHED and laced his hands behind his head as he leaned back against the cushions. "That kind of busts my theory about Thunder being the killer and him using his own eyedrops."

"Maybe Ann brought her own," I said, shrugging. "It's a common thing to carry. Did you interview Penny again?"

"No. She was hysterical. When she found out Stanley was dead, I thought we'd have to call an ambulance. I was afraid she was going to have a heart attack or something."

"Do you think it could've been an act?"

"Absolutely not," Adam said, standing

and stretching his arms over his head. "I've seen people fake sadness, and Penny had true, heart-wrenching grief—so difficult to watch. I actually wondered for a while if she had secretly loved Stanley all these years. It was the type of reaction I'd expect from Ann, not Stanley's secretary."

Based on what I'd seen at the funeral, Ann didn't suffer a lot of grief.

"And what about Ricky?" I asked.

Adam chuckled and cracked his knuckles. "I'm not happy with that guy. He's been avoiding us. I did wrangle a few thoughts out of him the day of the murder right after you left, but it isn't much."

"Can I read it?"

"Sure." He took the laptop from me and hit a few keys, then handed it back to me, shaking his head. "I can't believe how easy I'm finding it to give you access to police files. I could lose my job over this."

"It's a good thing I'm not going to tell anyone," I said. "I'm only trying to help and make you look like the superstar. That's all."

We exchanged smiles and I went back to reading.

· · ·

Deputy: Mr. Summers, how are you holding up?

Ricky: I'm fine. Surprised he's dead, but I'm fine.

Deputy: Can you tell us about your day? What time you arrived? What time you left after lunch?

Ricky: I guess I got in about nine-thirty. Not really sure. I'm not an early riser like Penny and Stanley and I like to get my morning workout in before I come to the office. Probably nine-thirty.

Deputy: And how was your morning?

Ricky: Uneventful. Lots of paperwork. I had morning appointments, lunch in the office then I met with a client.

Deputy: And who would that be?

Ricky: I'd rather not say. Client confidentiality.

I glanced up at Adam. "He didn't want to tell you he was representing Moonlit Coffin?"

He shook his head. "No, he didn't. I pieced it together with Penny and Ann's statement Moonlit Coffin was the client. Specifically, Thunder and another member."

"It wasn't Gunner?"

"No."

"You know, I heard him tell Ricky that they'd done what he wanted and now it was time for Ricky to take care of the case. That's why I thought he was involved in this."

Slowly pacing the floor in front of the fireplace, Adam pulled out his phone and typed. "I'm texting him to see when we can meet and I can find out what Moonlit Coffin did."

"If Gunner wasn't aware of Moonlit Coffin's involvement in the murder but then told Ricky that they'd done what he asked, it zeroes out the biker gang's involvement."

"Not necessarily," Adam said. "They may be talking about two different things. Thunder could've had someone else kill Stanley without informing Gunner."

"So you think that when Gunner told

Ricky they'd done what he'd asked, it was something else besides killing Stanley?"

"I do. Remember, Thunder was at the office before the murder and I wouldn't put it above Ricky to ask him to kill Stanley using his own eyedrops."

Very tricky and convoluted.

DEPUTY: *What happened after your meeting with the client?*

Ricky: *I had a dentist appointment, so I left.*

"DID YOU VERIFY THE DENTIST APPOINTMENT?" I asked.

"Yes, we did. He had a cleaning."

"Good thing he gets his chompers polished," Ruby said, matching her steps with Adam's. "You better make an appointment and get yours done, Bernie. It's been a while."

She wasn't wrong, but I hated going to the dentist almost as much as I disliked large crowds of people, so I put it off as long as possible.

· · ·

DEPUTY*: Then you returned to the office?*
Ricky*: Yes. And found you and that girl.*
Deputy*: Can you tell me about your rela-tionship with Stanley?*
Ricky*: He was my boss.*
Deputy*: Did you two get along?*
Ricky*: I've decided I'm not going to say any-thing else. I'd like my lawyer present when I speak to you again.*

"THAT'S IT?" I asked, setting down the computer.

"Yep. And now he and his lawyer are avoiding us, claiming to be too busy."

"That sounds fishy as heck. If he doesn't have anything to hide, why avoid speaking with the police?"

Adam shrugged. "Great question."

We stared at each other for a long moment, then I shut the laptop and set it on the coffee table.

A piece of the puzzle was missing.

Somehow, we'd overlooked the obvious, but I couldn't figure out what it could be.

Adam and I exchanged glances when my doorbell rang.

"Who's that?" Ruby asked. "Do you have a reservation you didn't tell me about?"

Picking up my phone, I shook my head. "Nothing." I moaned as I stood. "I hate walk-ins." Most of the time, they attempted to haggle me to lower my pricing. I preferred when people made reservations online and agreed to the set payment.

"Maybe it's a salesperson," Ruby replied as she followed me to the door. "If it's a walk-in, hold firm on your pricing! Don't let them talk you down! You still have to buy my ATV!"

"I won't," I muttered, mentally preparing to do battle with a haggler. Certainly I was the only person on this earth who'd agreed to buy an ATV for their ghost who loved to ride while alive...and in death.

Glancing through the window, I found Thunder and Gunner. With a gasp, I turned back to Adam. "It's Moonlit Coffin!" I hissed.

His eyes widened and he hurried over. "Which members?"

"Gunner and Thunder."

"Okay," he whispered. "I'm going to hide in the kitchen so I don't spook Thunder. Maybe he'll say something I can use to nail him. Gunner won't let anything happen to you."

There wasn't any time to discuss his plan. Another knock sounded and Adam hurried out of the room. I ran my sweaty hands over my jeans before opening the door.

"Can I help you?" I asked, keeping the door partially closed.

Thunder grinned as Gunner stared at me with his coal-black gaze. "We wanted to make sure you didn't have any further questions about our involvement in Stanley's murder," he said. "We wouldn't want you going to the police or anything."

Speaking of which...where had Adam parked his sheriff's cruiser? Yes, he'd followed me home, but I hadn't been focused on where he'd left it. As I peered between the two hulking men, I didn't see the car out front. They'd never have come to the door if it had been. If the two bikers decided to go around to the back of my house for whatever reason, would they find it there? Leading Thunder to believe I was already working for the police?

"I don't believe you're involved," I said, glancing at Gunner, who crossed his arms over his chest and became more menacing with every second.

"Let's go inside and discuss it," Thunder said, pushing open the door and striding past me.

"This boy has no manners," Ruby murmured as he walked right through her.

"Nice place," Thunder said as he took in the high ceilings, bright windows, fireplace and the sweeping staircase. "It would be a shame for anything to happen to you in here. Wouldn't want to make a mess. Blood's really hard to clean out of carpet and hardwood."

Gunner chuckled and kept his stare on me. I now knew he was undercover, but his laugh made me nervous. How far would he allow Thunder to take the intimidation? Was he really on my side?

"Don't you threaten my granddaughter, you big bully!" Ruby yelled. "And to think I used to drink tequila with this monster!"

As Thunder approached me, I blurted, "You knew my grandmother." This would either be a bonding moment or he'd hate me even more.

He narrowed his blue gaze on me. "I did?"

"Yes. Ruby. You used to hang out with her at Jezebel's place. Tip 'Em Back."

Recognition flickered in his eyes but his features didn't soften. "Fun lady. But back to business. Do you still think we're involved in Stanley's death?"

I shook my head. "No, I don't. I believe his wife has something to do with it, though." I really didn't know what to think, but I'd say the sky was purple and a pack of zombies had murdered the lawyer if it meant Thunder would back off and I didn't fear for my safety.

"Good girl," he said, standing in front of me and glaring down at me. The urge to back away was strong, but I held my ground. Thunder didn't know it, but I had two cops in my house. If he tried to hurt me, at least one of them would come to my rescue. I hoped.

"Can you please get out of my house now?" I asked. "I don't like feeling threatened." I glanced over at Gunner who smirked ever so slightly. Was he impressed with my bravery or laughing at my act?

"Yeah, get out of here, you greasy loser!" Ruby yelled. "If I were alive, I'd give you a one-two punch and bury your body in the desert! No one messes with my granddaughter!"

Ruby shadowboxed his face.

"I smell weed," Thunder muttered. "Are you in the drug trade, sweetie?"

"No. Now, please leave my house." I pointed at the front door and gave him my best I-mean-business glare even though my knees felt like Jell-O and they wanted to buckle, taking me to the floor.

He chuckled and slowly moved toward the exit, Gunner in tow. After placing his hand on the knob, he turned to me. "Just remember this: if the cops come sniffing around asking about the murder, I know who to blame. And I know where you live."

"Is that a threat?" I asked, now angry.

"It's a promise, little girl."

"Get out before I call the cops and have you arrested for trespassing."

"That's my girl! Don't take any of his nonsense!" Ruby yelled, still boxing the back of his head. "This guy was obviously dropped as a baby!"

As they walked out the door, Gunner gave me a slight smile and a nod. What the heck did that mean? I'd passed the test?

The roar of their bikes was a pleasant sound and I slumped against the door.

"Good job, honey," Ruby said. "Way to stand your ground."

"Are you okay?" Adam asked, hurrying around the corner. Placing his hands on my shoulders, he glanced at me from head-to-toe as if searching for the blood Thunder had mentioned.

"Yes. I'm fine. Scared, but he didn't touch me."

Adam sighed and wrapped me in a tight

embrace. After a moment, he led me over to the couch and we sat down.

"I'll tell you one thing," he said, his voice quiet with anger. "That guy is going down. If not for the murder, we're going to nail him for something else. But I'm hoping it's murder."

CHAPTER 18

THE NEXT DAY I arrived at Jezebel's for my self-defense class. Once again I'd tossed and turned the night away thinking of all the snappy comebacks I could've given Thunder if I'd had the ability to think on my feet and how I'd liked to have bloodied his nose for calling me 'little girl.' Condescending jerk.

I flung open the door and pulled off my sunglasses. Ruby spun around in a circle then yelled, "Jezebel! I'm heeerrreeee!"

My eyes adjusted a moment later and I scanned the empty bar. Chairs had been placed on top of tables, the jukebox stood quietly in the corner. The place of happiness and revelry I'd witnessed the other night was now hollowed and empty. "Jezebel?" I said out loud, fully expecting her to emerge from the office. I slipped off my coat and headed for the back room where she taught our classes.

I rounded the corner to find Gunner sitting in a chair stroking his thick black beard. Dressed in jeans, a black T-shirt, and his biker cut, the dim lighting reflected off his bald head. Mean and menacing were the only words I could use to describe his appearance. With a gasp, I backpedaled and almost made it out of the room. "Come sit, Bernie," he said, his deep voice rumbling through the quiet. "I'm not going to hurt you."

My gaze darted around the room from the folded-up table against the far wall to the dark shadows of the corners. "Is Thunder here?" I asked.

He shook his head. "Jezebel will be out in a minute. She's using the restroom. Come in and sit. We'll wait for her."

I nodded and approached on wobbly legs and sat down across from him. I knew he was a cop and that I should trust him, but just being in his presence made me uneasy.

"Is Ruby here with you?" he asked as his gaze darted around me.

"You betcha, big guy!" Ruby yelled.

"She is," I said. "Did Jezebel tell you about her?"

He nodded. "I liked your grandma. We used to do tequila shots together when she came to the bar. She and Jezebel's grandma, Janis… those two were hysterical together." He chuckled and shook his head while I noted that he talked about my ghost with such ease, I couldn't help but wonder if he'd had some interactions with a spirit trapped on this plane. "This one time, they got on top of the pool table and—"

"What are you doing here, Gunner?" I asked, in no mood to hear about Ruby's antics. "I'm supposed to meet Jezebel for a self-defense class."

He sighed and rubbed his face, his hands as big as catcher's mitts. "I wanted to see you. First to apologize for the other night out in the parking lot. I couldn't tell you who I was but I wanted to make sure you stayed clear of Thunder. He's bad news, Bernie."

"I realize that. And you also convinced me you were, as well. You scared me to death."

"Well, at least I got my point across. It was for your own protection."

"I understand that now, but I sure didn't then," I muttered.

"And I also wanted to apologize for showing up at your house yesterday. I tried to talk Thunder out of it, but he has it in his mind that you're going to snitch on him and he's going to be put away for Stanley's murder."

"Did he do it?"

Gunner shrugged. "I have no idea. If he did, or if he gave the order to have it done, I know nothing about it."

"He obviously feels very threatened by me, which only makes him look guilty."

"Do you have information pointing to him?"

"I'm clueless about Thunder," I said. "It was *you* who I thought killed Stanley."

"Really? Why me?" he asked, furrowing his brow.

"When I went back to Stanley's office, you were there speaking to Ricky Summers. I heard you tell him, *we did what you asked us to,* and I assumed that meant Moonlit Coffin had murdered Stanley for him and so you wanted payback."

"I thought you'd left the office?"

"Well, I had, but then I snuck back in to eavesdrop."

Gunner leaned forward and placed his elbows on his knees, then set his head in his hands, while uttering a curse. After a moment, he sat back again and crossed his arms over his chest. "There's fine line between bravery and stupidity, Bernie. Please keep that in mind and tread carefully."

Adam obviously hadn't had a chance to talk to Gunner since our discussion the prior day or I wouldn't have to explain myself.

"So, what did Moonlit Coffin do for Ricky?" I asked.

"We moved furniture for him," Gunner replied. "He bought a house and we took his stuff from his apartment to the new house. He's prospecting the club."

I snorted and shook my head. "It seems he'll fit right in with a bunch of law break-ers. You know he's a murder suspect, right?"

Gunner nodded. "Yeah, I do. And just so we're clear, most of the MC are law-abiding citizens. There are a couple who need to be weeded out, but overall, it's a good group of guys who want to hang out, do nice things for the community, and ride bikes. Thunder will be taken down at any time now and the rest of the turds in the punchbowl will go with him."

Frankly, I wasn't sure if I believed Gunner or not. Although Darla had had positive interactions with the MC, my rela-tions had been downright scary. "What case did you want Ricky to make go away?"

"There's one guy… he hit his old lady and she's pressing charges. I suggested we use Ricky—"

"You're trying to get a wife-beater off?" I shrieked. "How can you sleep at night?"

He held up his hands in front of him. "No, just listen, Bernie. I wanted to use Ricky as the lawyer because he's a dumb, self-centered jerk and is a prospect to the MC. Anyone who spends five minutes with the guy knows he's not cut out for any type of criminal law work. I figured we'd lean on him to clear the case, he'd fail, and he'd get booted out of Moonlit Coffin. I don't want him around."

"You're using him because you know he's a horrible lawyer and won't get the abuser off? And when he doesn't, Moonlit Coffin won't want him anymore?"

"In a nutshell, yes."

Talk about manipulation, backstabbing, and sleight of hand. I stared at the big man, my mouth agape. It seemed so much easier to be truthful and simply tell Ricky he wasn't club material, but what did I know about prospecting a MC? "Do you think he murdered Stanley?"

"I don't know, Bernie," he replied, shrugging. "It's a possibility. He's always said Stanley held him back from his true calling, and from what I understand, he can do what he wants with the law office now."

A door opened and shut in the back and Jezebel strode into the room on powerful legs wearing shorts and a sweatshirt covering her tattoo sleeve. "Hey, Bernie!" she called as she pulled her long blonde hair up into a ponytail and secured it with a rubber band. "How's it going, girl?"

"I'm fine," I muttered as I eyed Gunner, not feeling anywhere near fine.

"Hey, Jezzy!" Ruby said. "I'm really envious of everyone who hasn't met you!"

Grinding my jaw, I kept my focus on the undercover cop. Was he telling the truth about everything, or was I another pawn in his chessboard of life? He seemed to be scheming to move a lot of pieces, each one hopefully performing the way he wanted.

"Tell her!" Ruby yelled. "You're going to ruin it!"

Why those two insisted on trading insults, I'd never understand. I repeated Ruby's.

Jezebel snickered. "Ruby, weren't you

born on a highway? That's where most accidents happen."

Gunner laughed and shook his head. "I remember they did that when Ruby was alive."

"You don't seem too concerned that Jezebel and I are speaking to a dead woman," I said.

"I'm not. After seeing what humans are capable of, I have no right to think they aren't clever enough to come back after death."

Glancing over at Jezebel I noted the hesitation in her gaze. Was she worried about me being upset that Gunner was an undercover cop and she hadn't informed me? Or that I'd been blindsided by his presence during our self-defense class?

"I tried to get you to back off," she said softly. "I'm so sorry you got mixed up in this."

"Me, too," I said. "I should have listened to you."

"Bring it in?" Jezebel asked with her arms out wide. I stood and tripped over the leg of my chair, falling into her embrace.

"Your middle name should've been Grace," Jezebel said with a laugh as she slapped me on the back. "You ready to kick some butt?"

A deep blush crawled up my neck and into my cheeks. "I suppose so." Glancing over at Gunner, I willed him gone. Him observing my self-defense failure at the hands of Jezebel didn't sit well with me. I liked to suffer my shame with as few witnesses as possible.

Jezebel threw me a jump rope and we began the workout. Gunner eyed us with a slight smile on his face. I attempted to ignore him, figuring he was laughing at me as I tried to keep up with his very athletic girlfriend.

After the warm-up, Jezebel and I squared off as Ruby cheered me on.

"Let's see some kung-fu fighting!" she yelled as she punched the air.

It didn't take long for Jezebel to take me to the floor. As she straddled me, she pulled her fist back as though about to slam it into my face. Of course, she wouldn't, but she tried to make the training as realistic as possible.

"What's going on in here?" a deep voice rumbled from the doorway.

Jezebel's eyes widened as her gaze met mine and she whispered a curse.

"Uh oh," Ruby said. "Trouble with a capital T has arrived. And he goes by Thunder."

"Don't let me stop you from beating the snot out of that snitch."

I glanced over to find him leaning against the wall wearing a smirk along with his jeans, a blue T-shirt, and his cut. He ran a hand through his long blond hair as panic gripped my chest.

"Oh, no," I whispered.

"What are you doing here, man?" Gunner said, strolling over to him. "I thought you were at the clubhouse."

"You mentioned you were going to see Jezebel and thought I'd follow you over. I never imagined I'd walk in on her beating up someone."

The two shook hands as Jezebel slid off me, placing herself between me and Thunder. "I forgot to lock the front door after you arrived," she hissed. "This is bad. Very, very bad."

"This is worse than bad," Ruby yelled, throwing her hands up in the air. "If that guy lays a hand on Bernie, you and Gunner *will* protect her, Jezebel! He wants to bury her in the desert with all the other bodies!"

The fact that Ruby used her full name instead of a nickname—she meant business. And… other bodies? How was Ruby aware there were bodies buried out in the desert? And did I really want to know?

"Don't let me stop you," Thunder said as Gunner took his place at his side. "What did you uncover for her to deserve a beatdown?"

My heart wanted to beat out the front of my chest while fear caused my throat to constrict. I sat up and Jezebel and I exchanged worried glances while Gunner answered. "You said you wanted to be sure she wouldn't go to the cops, and I don't like to hit women. Decided to let my old lady take care of it."

"Good idea," Thunder said, chuckling. "Get on with it, Jezebel!"

She turned to me, her eyes wide with dread. "Run!" she mouthed.

I didn't have to be told twice. My flight instinct flew into high gear as I scrambled to my feet and took off for the door she'd come in from. It would lead me to the back of the building, where I'd never been. Ruby floated behind me screaming at the top of her lungs tethered by our leash, having been caught off guard.

Jezebel's footsteps sounded behind me as I skidded around the corner into a back hallway. If I ran to the right, it would take me to the main bar area. To the left… I had no idea, but it would be away from Thunder and that's all that mattered.

I ran down the hall and Jezebel caught up with me. "In here!" she hissed, opening a closet door. "Don't move!"

As I crammed myself in with a bucket and mop, cases of paper towels, toilet paper and bottles of booze, I took some deep breaths and tried to ignore the claustrophobia quickly engulfing me.

"She ran out the back door!" Jezebel

called out. Oh, my word. *What if Thunder found me?* I was a sitting duck.

Gunner and Thunder's deep voices carried into the hallway, but I couldn't make out what was said.

"Trouble is brewing," Ruby said from the other side of the door. "The police are here. They're sneaking in the back."

I gasped and placed my hand over my mouth.

"Just keep quiet, Bernie. They've got their guns drawn and they're being super sneaky."

Trembling from head-to-toe, I longed to sit down but there wasn't any room.

"I count six, including your favorite copper," Ruby said. "And he looks angry enough to chew nails."

Seconds later, someone yelled, "Freeze! Police! On the ground!"

A lot of shouting and swearing ensued and I shut my eyes, hoping no one had to shoot anyone. After a few minutes, Ruby poked her head through the door. "I think they got Thunder. I can't see anything, but it sounds like it. Gunner wasn't lying when he said the jerk would be going down soon. He was literally talking minutes." She shook her head. "Imagine that."

Did I step out of my hiding space or remain put and wait for Jezebel to fetch me?

As I debated what to do, I chewed my thumbnail and tried not to breathe too loudly. I didn't want to be a distraction if there was a problem arresting Thunder, but I also felt like I may suffocate in the cramped, dark space. Ruby was no help since she couldn't move more than fifteen feet away from me.

"She's in here," Jezebel said. "She's fine."

Footsteps sounded down the hallway and I slowly opened the door and looked to my left. Thunder was being led away in cuffs. To my right, Gunner walked toward me, also cuffed, a cop at his side. With a grin, he winked at me. Jezebel and Adam followed.

As our gazes met, relief swept Adam's face before he took me in an embrace.

"I was so worried when I saw your car in the parking lot," he whispered. "I thought Thunder had gotten to you."

"Thanks to Jezebel, no, he didn't," I whispered.

Adam sighed and held me tighter. "It's over," he said. "We've got him."

Sedona's residents could rest easy… another murder solved.

CHAPTER 19

I QUICKLY LEARNED that Adam hadn't meant they'd arrested Thunder for murder, but for being part of a drug ring spanning four states. Despite my unintended involvement, the police had finally gathered enough evidence to put the man in prison, mainly thanks to Gunner's long period undercover.

"So why did they take Gunner away in cuffs?" I asked Adam the next day as we waited in line at Canyon Coffee, which reminded me of a cozy living room with its overstuffed leather couches, magazine racks, and the fireplace in the middle of the store. I'd convinced Ruby to stay home so I could have a little time alone with him.

Thankfully, she'd readily agreed, even though she whined and sulked about it.

"We had to keep up the ruse of Gunner being a bad guy. Utah wants to extradite Thunder immediately since that's the main hub of the drug ring, so he'll never know that his second in command was the one who got him arrested."

"And what does Gunner do now?" I asked.

"Hopefully shave that god-awful beard." Adam gave a low laugh.

I tried to imagine Gunner clean-shaven, and drew a blank. "I bet Jezebel's happy he's finally out of that situation. It was so dangerous."

"For sure. That's a lot of weighted knowledge and worry for her to carry around for so many years. Gunner's done with undercover work in this area. At least now they can enjoy each other without the secret hanging over their heads."

"Do you think they'll be able to prove Thunder also killed Stanley?" I asked.

Adam shrugged. "I don't know. We've got his potential motive, Ricky asking him to do it, and the fact he carried eyedrops everywhere he went. We just don't have a confession."

"What if Ricky was the mastermind? Wouldn't it be best to put him away for the killing?"

"Oh, yeah. But first we've got to get Thunder to admit to the crime and finger Ricky as the instigator. We're trying to work out a deal where he gets less time for the drug ring in exchange for information on the murder."

"Well, I hope they nail them both," I muttered.

Glancing around the shop, I noticed Ann and Penny sitting together at a table in the corner. Penny wiped her face with a napkin as if she was crying while Ann reached across and squeezed her hand. "I'm going to say hello," I said, gesturing toward the two women.

"Hurry back."

I gave Adam a quick kiss and weaved through the tables toward the two women. Both smiled when they noticed me.

"Hi, Bernie," Penny said, dabbing her eyes once again. "How're things with you?"

"I'm fine," I replied. "What about you? Are you going to be okay, Penny?"

She nodded. "Eventually. My life is in such upheaval right now. First losing Stanley, then my job… I don't have any grounding. I need to find my purpose again."

Ann smiled warmly. "You're going to land on your feet. Don't worry."

I couldn't help but notice how Ann seemed far less upset than Penny about her husband's death. But then, I knew Ann's marriage had been different and she now had the freedom to do as she pleased… all the things Stanley had never wanted to do.

Maybe Ann should be looked at a little more closely.

"Ricky called me," Penny said. "He wants me to come back and help. Apparently, the new secretary isn't working out well for him."

Based on what Ruby had seen, that wasn't a surprise. It seemed Ricky had hired her for her looks rather than her skills.

"He says she doesn't know how to run a

law office like I did."

"Wow," I said. "I never expected to hear that. What did you tell him?"

Penny smiled so broadly, her cheeks almost pushed her eyes closed. "I told him to go shoot up more steroids. I'd rather have a mammogram every day than to work for him again. Did you know he called me a dinosaur to my face because I like to use a paper calendar instead of an online one? The nerve of that imbecile."

I chuckled at her hatred for the man, but also admired her for standing her ground. "Have you decided what you're going to do? Retire? Find a new job?"

"Ann and I were just discussing it," Penny said, glancing over at Stanley's wife. "We're both feeling a little lost right now."

We chatted a few more minutes and I went back to Adam after he placed our orders.

"Did you get me a scone as well?" I asked, linking my arm through his.

"I didn't. Go ahead and pick one. When the barista comes back, she can add it to the ticket."

As I debated between the cherry and the chocolate, I also considered Christmas. I wanted to have a party. Nothing too big— just close friends. Ruby would fight me over the plan. In her book, the more the merrier. In mine, the more people around, the higher my discomfort levels.

The barista returned with our coffee and I added a chocolate scone to the order. As I picked up the cup she'd set in front of me, she furrowed her brow. "Wait a minute," she said. "I think I got those mixed up."

I smelled my cup, and sure enough, Adam held my vanilla latte and I had his black cinnamon coffee.

"Sorry about that," she said, sighing. "We've been slammed today and my brain's not working."

"It's not a big deal," Adam replied, then handed her a five-dollar tip. "Have a good rest of your day."

She thanked him profusely and we turned to weave our way through the store to an empty table. As I sat down, I glanced up and noted Ricky had walked in. He got in line, then he spotted Penny and Ann.

After heading over to them, he set his palms on the table and spoke to Penny. Domineering was the word that came to my mind.

I nudged Adam. "Take a look at Penny and Ann."

As Penny's face turned a shade of purple that made me wonder if she was stroking out, she took a swing at him. He stepped away, shook his head, and returned to the line.

"She sure hates him," I muttered, taking a sip of my latte.

"Yes, she does," Adam agreed. "Thought I was going to have to step in there for a moment and break-up a fistfight."

I set down my cup and stared at it. Something bothered me, but I couldn't place what it was. The latte tasted fine—delicious, in fact. I glanced over at Adam. "How's your coffee?"

"It's really tasty. Glad we got the cup mix-up fixed before your latte ruined the taste of all this cinnamon goodness for me," he replied, winking.

I nodded absently, still glaring at his cup, trying to decipher what was wrong.

Was there something I wanted to tell Adam, and it had escaped my thoughts? No, it was about the coffee cups.

I let my gaze travel around the store, settling first on the barista who was wiping down a table, then on Ricky who now stood at the front of the line placing his order. Penny and Ann continued to remain seated, chatting away.

"What's wrong, Bernie?" Adam asked. "Is your latte bad? Are you feeling okay?"

I held up my finger, my revelation just on the cusp of consciousness. When it came to me, I gasped and placed my hand over my mouth. Finally, I met Adam's gaze.

"What is it?"

"I think I know who killed Stanley. Maybe. It's a crazy idea… but it makes sense."

"Tell me what you're thinking."

My heart thundered in my chest as I glanced over at Ann and Penny again, then at Ricky.

"What if the poisoned coffee wasn't supposed to go to Stanley?" I asked. "What if Ricky was the one who should've drunk it?"

Adam stared at me a long moment, his gaze flickering with uncertainty.

"Here me out," I said, holding up my index finger. "Let me finish."

"Okay, go ahead."

"Who among the suspects had a problem with Stanley?"

Adam sighed and nodded. "Well, his wife wasn't happy. Ricky was fighting with him about the changes in the office."

"Exactly."

"He'd broken off his relationship with Merry at Joyous Jewels. You said she hated Stanley so much, she wrote down in her diary that she wanted him dead."

"Yes. You're right. Now answer me this. Do you think any of them hated Stanley enough to actually kill him, or do you think all those reasons are pretty lame?"

"I'm not sure."

"Ann may be glad her husband's dead, but did she kill him? They're in their seventies. He's like another limb to her."

"True."

"And Ricky... yes, he has a lot to gain, but let's face it. Is he smart enough to pull it off? Is having his own practice worth killing over?"

Adam shrugged and narrowed his gaze. "People have killed for a lot less. What are you getting at?"

I sighed deeply, almost embarrassed to speak my theory. "Who has a problem with Ricky?"

Both our gazes slid across the shop. "Penny," he replied.

"He's been a thorn in her side since he began working there," I said. "He's been rude and condescending to her and a jerk to Stanley, who she obviously adored. Without him, she could go back to her regular life: she and Stanley in the office with no one else to bother her."

Adam's eyes widened. "You think the coffee was supposed to be for Ricky?"

"I do," I said. "Penny made the coffee and poured two cups. She's admitted that. Ann took one of the cups to Stanley's office."

"But she grabbed the wrong one," Adam whispered.

"Maybe? That's what I'm thinking."

We sat in silence for a long while as Adam processed my theory and we stared at Ann and Penny.

"I need to ask her about it." He took a long sip and stood. "What you've said does make sense."

Taking a deep breath, I followed him over to the table. The two women eyed him warily as he attempted to exchange pleasantries, but they answered curtly. I didn't blame them. Adam had interviewed both and made it known he considered them murder suspects.

He grabbed a chair from an empty table, pulled it over, and sat down. He smiled at Penny. "I saw you earlier when Ricky came in. You sure don't like him."

"Are you here chatting with me or is this part of your investigation?" Penny asked.

"A little of both," he said with a shrug. "Ricky's not a nice guy and I saw you take a swing at him. What did he say to you?"

Penny traded glances with Ann, then replied, "He called me a fat cow because I wouldn't go back to work for him."

Dang. I would have swung at him as well.

Adam shook his head. "Wish I could arrest him for being rude, but unfortunately, I can't. Can I ask you one more question, and then I'll be on my way?"

Penny nodded. "What is it?"

"The day Stanley died, you made two cups of coffee after lunch, correct?"

"Yes."

"And then Ann came into the kitchen and took one from you."

"Correct. I gave the other one to Ricky."

Adam glanced over at me, then back at Penny. "Is it possible that you were the one who poisoned the coffee? That it was meant for Ricky, and Ann grabbed it and gave it Stanley?"

Ann gasped while Penny's face paled and tears welled in her eyes. "Of course not!" she whispered. "What an obscene thing to say."

Her words may have indicated innocence, but her body language showed otherwise. She lifted her cup with shaky hands, took a short drink, then set it down.

"Penny, is this true?" Ann asked. "Did I

give Stanley the poisoned coffee?"

For a long moment, Penny remained silent and stared at the table. Finally, she straightened her shoulders and gazed at Ann, a lone tear tracking down her cheek. "Yes. I did it. I wanted to get rid of Ricky. He's so difficult. He brought so much stress to Stanley. He's rude and belligerent. I wanted to go back to the days when it was just Stanley and me, and I thought if Ricky died, the police would think he overdosed on his steroids, or they caused him to have a heart attack. They'd never expect I would poison him."

And they probably wouldn't. No one had suspected the sweet grandma with Stanley's death.

"I'd never hurt Stanley," she said, meeting Ann's gaze. "You came right after I had added the eyedrops and I became so flustered. I wanted to kill a man and you wanted to chitchat. Then you took a cup, and I wasn't sure if you grabbed… the one with the eyedrops or not. I couldn't admit I was trying to poison Ricky, so I just prayed you'd delivered Stanley the correct one."

"Then you left the office," I said.

"Yes. I became so upset and stressed out, I had to leave. When I returned and discovered Stanley had been killed… I… I can't describe the depths of my grief."

If I recalled correctly, Adam had referred to her as hysterical.

Glancing over at Ann, I tried to gauge her thoughts. She stared at Penny, her mouth slightly open, but her eyes remained dry. "I'm suddenly not feeling well," she whispered. "I'd like to go home, if you don't mind, Deputy."

Adam stood. "Of course."

"I'm so sorry, Ann!" Penny wailed, now in a full frenzy. "I didn't mean to do it!"

Ann laid her hand on Penny's shoulder. "I know you didn't. The thing is, many times during my marriage I fantasized about murdering Stanley simply because I wasn't enough for him. Somehow, I'd do it without being caught. My method would be sly and devious. Perhaps, undetectable. The irony is, my fantasy came true. I killed him and didn't even realize it."

CHAPTER 20

ADAM TOOK Penny down to the station and I returned home with a smug smile and feeling pretty good about myself. That changed when Ruby met me at the back door with her hands on her hips, her mouth pursed into a fine line.

"What's wrong?" I asked.

"That new neighbor moved in today, but she has to go."

I slipped off my coat and hung it on the peg by the door. "Why is that?"

"Because she's more annoying than a pimple on a butt cheek!" Ruby yelled, throwing her hand up in the air. "She's been here three times since you left.

How long have you been gone? Two hours?"

Never having had a pimple on my butt cheek, I wasn't aware of the level of aggravation they could cause. But based on Ruby's rantings, they must be highly frustrating. "What does she want?" I asked, walking into the kitchen.

"How the heck am I supposed to know?" she growled. "It's not like I can answer the door and question her!"

"Would you please calm down?" I asked.

"No. I won't."

"Well, I have good news. I solved Stanley's murder."

Her eyes widened as she clapped her hands, my new annoying neighbor apparently forgotten. "Tell me more! Wait! Let me guess. Was it Ann? I figured. No, it was Ricky, wasn't it? He had Thunder do it?"

I shook my head and grinned. "Penny did it."

Ruby stared at me a long moment then narrowed her gaze. "You're joking. No way."

"Yup. She confessed to it all."

"But she loved Stanley!"

I fetched a glass of water and sat down at the island. "Yes, she did, and she never meant to kill him. However, the coffee with the eyedrops was meant for Ricky and Ann happened to grab that cup and serve it to Stanley."

With a gasp, Ruby placed her hand over her mouth. "Well, well, well. I never saw that one coming. How did you figure it out? What clue did we miss?"

"Nothing," I said with a shrug. "The barista mixed up my coffee with Adam's and the theory just came to me. We asked Penny about it, and she admitted it."

"Unbelievable. Well done, Bernie. Although I wish I could've been there to see it all go down."

"It honestly wasn't very exciting," I said. "There wasn't any drama, no fighting… just Penny quietly admitting that she killed Stanley. But Ann was there."

Ruby and I discussed the happenings a little longer, then the doorbell rang.

"That's probably the new neighbor," she grumbled. "Go see what she wants and tell her she has snakes living in her attic. Maybe she'll leave the 'hood."

With a sigh, I walked through the big house, making mental notes of everything I had to do. With four people checking in tomorrow, I had better phone Darla and give her the heads up so she could prepare breakfast for my guests in the coming days. I also needed to stock my wine stash and do a last-minute inspection of my guest rooms. Checking my toilet paper supply wouldn't be a bad idea, either.

I opened the front door to find a middle-aged woman with a blonde bob smiling at me dressed in jeans and a red shirt.

"Can I help you?" I asked.

"Yes! I just moved in across the street," she said, sticking out her hand. "Since no one in the neighborhood has come to welcome me, I thought I'd go door-to-door and introduce myself!"

I took her palm in mine, wondering how I'd missed that etiquette point, especially considering her house had been empty until today. "It's nice to meet you. I'm Bernie."

"Sylvia!"

"Welcome to the neighborhood."

"With how annoying she is, she should've been named Karen," Ruby muttered.

"Would you like to come in?" I asked, ignoring my ghost.

"Sure! Just for a bit. I can't stay."

"Moving's a big job," I said stepping aside to allow her to pass. "Lots of unpacking, I'm sure."

"Not really," she said, glancing around. "My husband and I just divorced and I only took what I needed. So glad to be rid of him. Thankfully, we didn't have kids. Well, he didn't have kids with me anyway. He did with some floozy in Flagstaff."

I arched an eyebrow and glanced over at Ruby.

"Way too much information," Ruby said, shaking her head. "However, she may prove to be quite entertaining. Or horribly annoying. I guess that remains to be seen."

"This is a beautiful home," Sylvia said.

"Of course it is," Ruby replied. "I built the darned thing."

The tall ceiling, the fireplace, the sweeping staircase and all the windows made for a stunning living room. "Thank you," I said.

"I'm a nurse at the medical center," Karen continued as she sat down on one couch while I took a seat across from her on the other.

"How long have you been there?"

"Ten years," she said. "I understand you run a bed and breakfast?"

"Yes."

"I wish I would've known that before I moved in."

"Why is that?" I narrowed my gaze on her.

"Because this is a residential neighborhood. I expect peace and quiet. Not a hotel with people coming and going at all hours of the day and night. And I like to be acquainted with my neighbors so I can call the police if I see any strange faces."

"Well, I only have three rooms to rent, so it's nothing like a hotel," I replied. "And my guests are usually very quiet."

"Yeah, especially the guy who bit it in the

upstairs bedroom," Ruby said with chuckle. "He was the quietest of them all!"

"I've never had any trouble," I continued. "You don't have anything to worry about with my business."

Sylvia eyed me for a moment, then nodded. "Well, that's good to hear, but I don't believe it for a second."

"Excuse me?"

"You're running a bed and breakfast in a residential neighborhood. That must be illegal."

Fisting my hands in my lap, I forced a smile. My new neighbor was revealing herself as a potential thorn in my side. "I have my proper permits. I'm not doing anything illegal."

"We'll see about that." She sighed and stood. "I just wanted to let you know I'm going to the city council to see about getting your business out of my neighborhood. It's just not right."

"With all due respect, I've been here for over three years," I said, also getting to my feet. "You just moved here. It's not *your* neighborhood. I've never had any complaints from any other neighbors."

"That may be the case, but that doesn't mean there won't be issues in the future. I'd like to avoid those."

I followed her to the door, my blood boiling as Ruby issued a string of curses and threats while trailing behind me. Things I wished I could say but never would, simply because I hated confrontation. Especially with a woman I'd known for less than ten minutes.

"My next stop is the neighbor two homes down on the left. Do you know his name?"

I wouldn't tell her even if I did. "No, sorry."

"Well, his tree out front really needs a trim. If a monsoon storm comes through and takes it down, it could block the road. Then, I'll be late for work, and we can't have that."

Of course we couldn't. God forbid something or someone inconvenienced Sylvia.

"It was nice meeting you, Bernie," she

said, smiling brightly. "I'm sure that once we get our differences straightened out, we'll become great friends."

Ruby snorted. "I doubt that, you snotty—"

"You won't be taking away my livelihood," I said. "I've operated my business without issue for years. Nothing you say is going to change that."

"We'll see."

Turning on her heel, she strolled down my walkway, then across the street to the neighbor. "Threatening someone isn't a good way to make friends!" I called after her, then slammed the door. "Can you believe her? Who does she think she is?"

"Beats me, but she's got a rude awakening coming if she thinks this neighborhood is going to stand for her demands." I didn't know many of the neighbors except to wave and smile as I drove by. Did any of them feel the same way about my business as Sylvia did? No one had ever mentioned anything to me, and my guests had always been quiet and respectful of my neighbors.

"When I was alive, I knew almost

everyone in this cul-de-sac," Ruby said. "We used to have block parties. You should start reaching out to them and getting to know them because you're going to need everyone on your side."

"Do you really think she'll go through with it? Trying to put me out of business?"

"I sure do. From what I've seen, a lot of the same people still live here from when I was alive. They're good souls, Bernie. Get them on your side. They won't want any part of her."

"How do you think I should go about doing that?"

As an introverted homebody, just the thought of introducing myself to a stranger who hadn't interacted with me first made my heart race and my palms sweat.

"I'm not sure," Ruby said, tapping her forefinger against her chin. "I know you won't go knock on a door to say hello. You'll need a reason for being there."

She understood me so well.

"I've got it! We'll make soap! Well, you'll make soap and you'll deliver it in cute gift bags for Christmas!"

"There's one issue," I said.

"What's that?"

"I've never made soap and I have no idea how to do so."

"You leave that to me," Ruby said. "I used to make it for Christmas gifts every year."

"I didn't know that."

Ruby shrugged. "You never came for Christmas."

"You never visited us, either," I said, following her into the kitchen.

"I did a couple of times when you were young. But your mom and I never got along. She's so dang strict and absolutely no fun."

No argument there. Being raised by her had caused my own regimented routines. Ruby was slowly unraveling them. Sometimes I was glad, but other times I wanted to return to the disciplined life. Especially when I discovered my pants no longer fit.

"So I make soap and deliver it to the neighbors," I said.

"Yes, and you talk to them. Woo them with your smile and sparkling personality. I guarantee you, if she's just moved in and she's on your doorstep the same day, she's going to be nothing but trouble for everyone. It's time to rally the neighborhood troops."

I nodded. Of course, Ruby was right. I needed everyone on my side to fight with me against the tyrannical "Karen" who'd moved in. She'd threatened to take away my livelihood. She was going door to door to introduce herself and complain about people's trees. As a community collective, we needed to shut her down. But first, I had to introduce myself to my fellow neighborhood warriors.

"So tell me now, how do I make soap?"

Sylvia would soon regret moving into this neighborhood.

The next novel in the Sedona Spirit Cozy Mysteries...

WHEN BERNIE'S horribly annoying neighbor is found dead, she's in the sheriff's crosshairs. Will Ruby and Bernie be able to discover the true killer before Bernie goes to prison for a crime she didn't commit? Find out in **The Neighbor is Nixed and...**

***

If you're looking for a little Christmas Spirit, you can grab the standalone novelette in the Sedona Spirit Cozy Mysteries, **Christmas is Canceled.**

Will Bernie's favorite time of year bring her joy... or tears?

ABOUT THE AUTHOR

Carly Winter is the pen name for a USA Today best-selling and award-winning romance author.

When not writing, she enjoys spending time with her family, reading and enjoying the fantastic Arizona weather (except summer - she doesn't like summer). She does like dogs, wine and chocolate and wishes Christmas happened twice a year.

To be notified of new releases, book recommendations, to learn more about Carly, for your chance to win giveaways and for more information on her books, please visit:
CarlyWinterCozyMysteries.com

Sedona Spirt Mysteries

Bernie and the ghost of her dead grandmother find themselves in the middle of various murder investigations. Danger and hilarity ensues as the crazy duo follow the clues to discover the killers.

The Tri-Town Murders

Complete Series

Follow newspaper reporter Tilly and her group of fun, quirky friends as they solve murders in a fictional, small town in California.

News and Nectarines

News and Nachos

News and Nutmeg

News and Noodles

Killer Skies Mysteries

Set in 1965, join Patty Briggs, stewardess extraordinaire, as she flies the skies and solves murders with the help of her friends… and one cute FBI agent!

9 781737 372424